BETWEEN WALLS OF WATER

RANDY ANDERSON

ISBN   978-1-953821-75-1 Ebook
ISBN   978-1-953821-76-8 Paperback

The EC Publishing LLC books may be ordered
through booksellers or by contacting:

EC Publishing LLC
116 South Magnolia Ave.
Suite 3, Unit F
Ocala, FL 34471, USA
Direct Line: +1 (352) 644-6538
Fax: +1 (800) 483-1813
http://www.ecpublishingllc.com/

Ordering Information:
Quantity sales. Special discounts are available on quantity purchases by corporations, associations, and others. For details, contact the publisher at the address above.

Printed in the United States of America

TABLE OF CONTENTS

ACKNOWLEDGEMENT

I WOULD LIKE TO THANK my Lord and Savior, Jesus, for His continued encouragement and ideas. It is a fact that I could not do this without Him in my life. I hope and pray that as you read this book, it may enlarge your vision of the Heavenly Father.

I would also like to give a special thank you to my wife Kathy, and our family for their love and support in pushing me to do my best.

I am honored that you chose to read this book. I hope you enjoy and grow from it.

INTRODUCTION

He stood on the shore of the Red Sea, looking out across the deep blue water, and waited. He was waiting on a God who was as new to him as those who had followed him out of Egypt. The people of Israel had been enslaved by the Egyptians for generations. They had been forced into hard, unrelenting labor at the hands of the Egyptian taskmasters.

He recalled the ten plagues brought upon Egypt because Pharaoh would not let the people go. The last plague was the most severe. It took the life of every firstborn in Egypt from man and animal—the only escape, The blood of a lamb on the doorpost. After the death of Pharaoh's own son, it was only then, he let the people go.

They were now trapped between the Egyptians and the Red Sea. Had this New God led them to this place to die? Moses stood looking out across the sea and in his heart, he could not see the true God, the God of their ancestors, turning on them. He believed in Him and trusted Him with all his heart, and he knew that Yahweh would not leave them to die. He would provide a way... Between Walls of Water.

CHAPTER 1

ACTS

Sharp, small pictures so real his muscles jumped and flinched as they passed through his mind. A black night starkly lit by the full moon. Cries in the darkness so close he felt them brush his skin. Black smoke moved snakelike through the shadows. Blood of a lamb dripped from a door. He felt the air dissipate from his lungs as the snake of mist slithered closer to his family's house. It stopped, whipping its undefined head toward him. A heartbeat of paralyzing fear passed, and then the mist-creature coiled and leaped forward, jaws gaping in a harsh hiss. He convulsed back and shut the door.

A voice punctured his vision. Joshua? Acts heard him faintly, but as a few moments passed he began to understand what Joshua was saying.

"Acts! Acts, are you well? Did you have another dream?"

"Yes," Acts groggily replied. He rubbed his face with both hands, slowly recognizing the desert sand he had grown newly accustomed to in the past week. "It seems I never know when one will happen."

"Did you feel anything before it came?" Joshua asked.

"Yes. It was that same ringing I heard the last time in my ear, first in one, and then in both," Acts replied.

Joshua leaned over and offered his hand as he had done many times before and pulled Acts to his feet. "I'm going to talk to Moses about this."

"No," Acts said quickly. "He… he has so much else to think about. I'm not hurt." A hesitant smile tweaked the corner of his mouth. "Maybe these mysterious dreams that show the past *do* have a lesson or two for the future." His smile blossomed weakly, pulling along his feeble attempt at humor. "But, still, they're just dreams. Anyway, I'm okay. Don't worry about me. Thanks for caring, though."

Joshua smiled. "All right, my brother. If you're ready, we have to be getting back so we can give report of our scouting to Moses."

"I'm fine and fit for duty, my captain." Acts called Joshua "captain" because Joshua was the one training him in battle techniques, decision-making, and teaching him how to handle stressful situations as a teenage boy. But he was more than a teacher; he was the older brother Acts never had. Even though there was a five-year age difference, Joshua looked at Acts as an equal and never belittled him, always remaining a patient teacher. Acts measured shoulder to shoulder with Joshua, but his frame still lacked the musculature of a grown man. To keep Acts' morale high, Joshua told the younger boy, "You are getting stronger every day." Acts thought in his heart Joshua treated him as Moses treated Joshua.

At the same time, though, Acts knew he was not immune to Joshua's anger. When Joshua did lose patience with Acts, he would first calm himself, then teach and explain the reason for his impatience; he'd even been known to apologize. Either way, it was always better than the way Acts' father and his siblings had treated him. His family also distrusted Moses, the man the Lord used to free them from Pharaoh, the King of Egypt.

~

The Lord God caused nine plagues to fall on Egypt, but Pharaoh hardened his heart toward the Hebrews in response. The Lord gave instructions to the Hebrews to put lambs' blood on the doorposts and over the doors of their houses, with the blood of the lentil dripping on the threshold of the door. The reason was for the protection of those inside the house. The Lord God was going to send the Destroyer through the land to kill all the firstborn of man and animal in Egypt. Only the presence of the blood promised safety. Even though it had only been a day since that night of terror, it still seemed Acts found himself peering into the darkness, feeling like a little boy despite his fifteen years.

That fateful night, Acts' curiosity urged him to look out the door when he saw a dark shadow pass across the full moon. Though its shape resembled a serpent, its form shifting in different shades of shadow and gray, glistening in the light of the moon. It moved as a mist in a soft breeze. He jumped when the first screams of surprise and grief echoed through the city. The sounds came from some distance, but to Acts, it felt like they originated next door. Time passed, and then the serpentine shadow turned down Acts street, and it began to weave between doors. By this time, the cries from the city were many and heavy with anguish, and the air was so saturated with death Acts could taste the metallic tang beneath his tongue. Some Hebrews had not done as Moses instructed and they too, lost their firstborn. The snake mist slowly advanced toward Acts' home, and when it reached him, it turned to face Acts. Although it possessed no discernable features, Acts felt its eyes burn through his and into his skull. Seeing it coil in preparation for a lunge, Acts jerked and slammed the door. His heart pounded, and fear gripped his throat. He could hardly move. He had witnessed Death. But death could not enter his father's house because of the lamb's blood on the doorpost. The essence of the absence of life had looked into his soul and desired him, even though it had already taken so many lives that very night.

"Get away from the door!" shouted a gruff and uncaring voice. "We are going to do just as Moses has said so we can get out of this prison."

Acts' father, Uebel, a man of very little patience and no sign of love toward the boy. He made it very clear he followed Moses, not because Moses was chosen by God, but because Moses was the way out of Egyptian slavery.

Acts was the youngest of nine children, the oldest of which was twenty years Acts' senior. After that brother came his oldest sister, then five more brothers, and then his sister Klee, who was only three years older than Acts. Klee had raised Acts because their mother had died in childbirth with him. That gave his father reason to hate Acts. Klee acted as a mother, sister, and best friend to Acts, and out of such a relationship formed the deepest of love and respect.

"Do you want your oldest brother to die, too?" demanded his father. "Now get over here with your sister and stop moving around."

Uebel spoke to him like he was a five-year-old, never acknowledging the independent and well-built teenager Acts had grown to be. Acts stood a full head taller than his father, and almost two heads above his sister. Yet it was in her arms he found parental security that night. They felt safe with each other; none of the other brothers or sisters still lived with them. They had their own families, but even so, they never included their youngest siblings. Now, Klee and Acts were their own family, and together they waited through that night as the Shadow of Death passed over them, just as Moses had said it would. Pharaoh had many wives and so many of his sons fell victim to this Death Angel because of his own pride. It weakened the heart of the King of Egypt to the point of letting the children of Israel leave.

Acts' thoughts floated back to the present. Joshua dusted the sand from Acts' back and picked up the spilled water skin, now only half full of water, and handed it to Acts. "Well, we'd better go back and get word to the runners, so Moses will know all is clear and no one follows." The Israelites had camped at Etham on the edge of the wilderness, and Moses had sent Acts and Joshua past the rear guard in order to follow the company and watch for any Egyptian troops that might appear to spy or even harm the last of the company.

They began a slow-paced run to catch up to the rear guard, which consisted of three tribes: Dan, Asher, and Naphtali. These were the tribes Moses had put in that place of honor. The first tribe they would come to was Naphtali.

The pillar of cloud that led them by day gave them shade from the heat of the sun. But still, the heat had gradually built up to an almost unbearable level when Acts and Joshua caught up to Ahira, the leader of Naphtali.

"Hoshea!" shouted Ahira. This was the name Joshua had until he became Moses' servant and Moses changed his name to Joshua. Even though some time had passed since then, some still called Joshua by his old name. Ahira shielded his eyes from the glare of the sun off the cloud that went before the entire company of Israel. As the young men approached, he questioned, "How did the scouting go?"

"Well," Joshua panted, coming to a stop and resting his hands on his knees, catching his breath. "No one in sight. Not even dust flying in the air."

Ahira smiled and slapped Joshua on the back. "Rest and eat. I will send word to Moses that you have returned safely and of the good word you and Acts bring."

Joshua straightened and offered a rolled piece of parchment to the tribal leader. "Please instruct the runner to take this message to Moses so he will know we are to come soon."

"Certainly," Ahira answered as he motioned for the runner to carry the message to the next runner. Each tribe had enough runners to move messages throughout the entire company.

Knowing the tribes were spaced about a mile apart and each tribe was in a wide oval shape that was approximately three miles in length, Joshua quickly calculated. This would mean covering several miles.

Acts, whose lungs had just quit burning, shot a surprised glance at Joshua for the short amount of time Joshua had given them to make such a distance in this heat. But Joshua played like he did not see Acts' stunned look. The younger one smirked and shook his head at his teacher's orneriness.

Fatigue pulled on both Joshua and Acts. They entered the cover of the front of the tent where they were brought water with which to wash and food to eat. They slept until the next morning and rose early to begin the journey to the front of the camp. Etham was on the edge of the desert, but plenty of grass clumped in the dirt for grazing, and watering holes were frequent finds. The company had camped here.

Acts looked over at Joshua who knew what his young companion was thinking. "I know it is a long distance each day, but I have thought about where we will rest tonight."

Acts sighed and asked, "How far in will we be by the end of the day?"

Joshua smiled and answered, "Your sister's tent," he said with some excitement.

Acts had not expected that. Seeing his sister would be a very good thing for him and it wouldn't be bad for Joshua either. Acts found a burst of energy and said, "Then we'd better get going, my captain!" Joshua smiled as they turned to begin the run for that day.

As they ran past the throng of people traveling within their tribes, Acts marveled at the number in this great assembly. He remembered the numbers called off by tribes according to their count of men twenty years and older capable of fighting. The total came to 603,550 overall, excluding women, children, and young men such as Acts. He had heard there were over two and a half million, in total. A sea of people, who had lived every day of their lives knowing exactly what lay ahead, were *now* walking into an unknown future.

Using every kind of craft, every area of expertise of which they could possibly conceive, from cloth to gold, the Hebrews had created a beautiful world for the Egyptians, a harsh and unrelenting people. Slavery was all that Acts had ever known, as did his father and his father before him. The bloodline went back generations to the man they knew as Jacob, whose name was changed to Israel. Jacob's son Joseph had been placed second in command of all Egypt. God had placed Joseph in that position so His people would not perish in a seven-year drought that the Lord brought. When Joseph and the good king of Egypt died, all the good he had brought fell into oblivion. The Egyptians took the Hebrews as slaves. For generations, the Hebrews served their Egyptian masters until their last breath. Freedom existed only as an idea in the minds of the Hebrew people.

They cried out to God for deliverance, never knowing what real independence could mean. Over time, the people of Israel had lost their relationship with The Only True God who had used Joseph in such a mighty way. Freedom and knowing 'The God of Abraham' was like someone describing a beautiful gem, that had never been seen.

Acts looked into the faces of the people as he passed, people smiling and laughing. Some would even stop their tasks and begin to jump around with joy. There was singing and dancing. It was a sight he never thought would be real.

They reached their own tribe of Ephraim and Acts immediately began looking for his sister's tent. He rounded the edge of their tent and saw her with a lamb in her arms. When Klee looked up and saw Acts running to her, she quickly set the lamb down and opened her arms to meet him. They embraced, squeezing all of the stress and struggle of the previous days away, and she began checking him over to see that he was alright.

"You look good, little brother, and does that smile on your face tell me that all went well?"

"Yes," he replied, hugging her again. "I missed you."

"As did I," came a tender but commanding voice. Joshua stood a small distance away, waiting for the right moment in the reunion of sister and brother to make his presence known.

"Joshua!" Klee blurted, startled. Acts stepped to her side with his arm over her shoulder. "You look..." she paused slightly, her face scrunched in thought, searching for the right words, "very...good... also," she stuttered rather awkwardly.

Joshua smiled and embraced her, but instead of letting her go, he held her, staring into her eyes. Acts, becoming uncomfortable, shifted his weight and cleared his throat.

Joshua looked over, surprised, like he had forgotten the younger man was standing there. Joshua released Klee and smoothed his tunic. "I should check in with my brothers, as well."

Klee said rather quickly before Joshua could get too far, "I will be cooking supper a little later. Would you like to eat with us?"

"I would like that very much!" Joshua answered. "I will be back soon." Turning to leave, Joshua stumbled over the lamb she had been holding, which caused brother and sister to giggle at the sight.

Later that evening, after a good meal and everyone was full, Joshua said, "I am going to stay with my parents tonight. Acts, I will come back to get you in the morning. You need to be ready early." Acts smiled with affirmation. Taking his leave, Joshua bowed to Klee, moving backward, almost tripping again over the same lamb. Recovering rather awkwardly, he quickly made his exit away from the chuckling of his favorite friends.

Klee and Acts talked as they both began cleaning up the dishes. As they reclined for the evening, there was so much to catch up on. Neither realized when they had drifted off to sleep.

Very early the next morning, Klee made breakfast for Acts. The fellowship had been sweet until the rough sound of his father's voice shattered the moment. He had returned from a long evening with people he called "friends" and smelled horrible.

"Well, the young scout returns." Sarcasm smeared through the sentence. "You *still* following in Joshua's shadow?"

"Yes, sir," Acts replied respectfully.

"You will never see who the real leader is, will you?"

"What do you mean?" asked Acts, even though he knew what came next.

Uebel puffed up. "Korah is the man who will take over when Moses is dead. He's a real leader."

Even though Acts did not agree or even think it possible, he kept quiet in order not to disrespect his father. The older man would eventually exhaust all his air, if he chose to continue speaking, and then leave them alone, so Acts waited.

Klee felt the tension and stood, setting her bowl aside. "Come see the three new lambs born just yesterday."

Acts gave her a silent glance of thanksgiving for removing him from a very uncomfortable situation.

They walked outside. She looked at him and told him, "With each passing day, he seems to become more and more bitter, even toward me," Klee commented when they passed out of earshot. "I don't understand what's happening to him, but the more time he spends with Korah and his two friends, Dathan and Abiram, the worse he becomes. Sometimes I'm afraid to come into the tent."

"You will not have to be afraid as long as I am near," Acts stated.

Klee smiled and gave him a hug. "Joshua will be back very soon."

"Not soon enough for you," he joked. Klee gave him a sisterly slap to the cheek.

Joshua arrived wearing the same grin he wore when he left earlier, though it faded to an indiscernible mask once he spotted Acts' father. Seeing Joshua return, Uebel spoke. "So, the teacher of the young warrior returns. You are wasting your time, Joshua; he will never be a warrior like his brothers."

"No, he won't," Joshua agreed bluntly. "He will be seven times the warrior and will possess the wisdom that goes with the ability."

Joshua never broke his gaze with Acts, and it made Uebel so angry that he retreated further back into the tent.

Klee smiled at Joshua. "Good answer."

They reached Moses' tent later that day, shortly after the sun had reached its highest point. Moses, a strong, tall, handsome man, stretched out his arms and took Joshua in as if he were his own child. "It's good to see you, my son." Moses' voice was strong and full of love, a greeting that Acts had always wanted, but never received from his own father. Moses turned to Acts and said, "And it's good to see you, Acts, 'the Acts of good will,'" and Moses gave him a bear hug, as well. Moses always called him "Acts of good will" because that was what Moses saw in Acts' heart.

"So, the n-news is no one follows?"

"No one follows, not even dust in the air," Joshua reported. Acts had a slight moment of déjà vu, and remembered where he heard it before.

"Good, good." Moses leaned on his staff in thought before speaking again. "I have met with the Lord God, and He has given instruction as to what the c-company is to do next."

Acts felt excitement and curiosity bubble to life within him, but he restrained the questions as Joshua asked, "What is His command, Moses?"

Moses took a step back and smiled. The Lord told me He is going to bring glory to His name and test the hearts of His people. I don't know all the Lord God has planned, but I can tell you where we are to go so that you, Joshua, my servant, can take the message to the leaders of the tribes. You will tell them we are to turn back to Pi Hahiroth between Migdol and the Red Sea."

An expression of complete surprise came over Joshua's face. "I don't mean to question you, Moses, but that is back toward Egypt. We could march through the land of the Philistines. The hearts of the people are high and ready for battle."

Moses held up a hand. "The Lord has told me that b-battle may change the minds of the people and make them want to go back to Egypt. This is not the way, Joshua. We must obey what the Lord God tells us and not trust what our eyes see. He is the only *true* God and He commands obedience. He is the One who controls our future, so we will do as He says and not question his Word, for it is there we find victory." Moses spoke to Joshua as a leader to his servant, but at the same time, teacher to student.

Joshua apologized. "Moses, I... I meant no disrespect to you or to the Lord God. With all my heart, I want to please Him, who has brought us out of the land of slavery. I am your servant and will do as you say."

The tension broke. Moses knew the heart of Joshua and how God had pointed him out to Moses as being special above all other men in the entire company.

Moses then turned to Acts and said, "Will you please go get us some fresh water from one of the water carts while I talk with Joshua?"

Acts understood they needed this time and so he answered with a smile, "Right away, Moses. I will get the water… and some dates!"

Moses laughed and said, "Yes, that would be good."

Moses turned back to Joshua and said, "Now, let's talk of how to turn all of these people around." He pulled out some parchment from his tent and, as they sat in the shade of the pillar of cloud, Moses took some ink and began to lay out the picture of how the task would be accomplished.

"Each tribe occupies a few miles of space in a 'somewhat' oval shape. I know, as we travel through the mountains, the tribes lengthen and then reform. There is about one mile between the tribes for distinction and to allow the ground to recover, so that is about 23 total miles in length. We have runners in each tribe that c-carry the flag of that tribe and men with flags on the edge of each tribe to keep them from spreading out too far. This is how we left Egypt in the way the Lord told me". Moses continued, "Now we will need a turning p-point because the tribes are to remain in the same order". Moses pointed to the large rock that was outside his tent by an underground spring at the oasis where they were camped. "That will be the first turning point. This rock will serve as the pivot of which the center of each tribe will make the first turn, just as soldiers turn in a march." Moses took his staff and held it in the middle parallel to the ground. "The staff is the tribe, and I am the rock." Moses then began to move the staff around his body showing Joshua how the tribe would turn. "Judah will start the turn first since they are to remain at the front of the company. The tribal leaders will be positioned at the front and center of each tribe with their banners held high so the people can see them. Each tribal leader will pass the rock and turn to the east. Have the women and children positioned to the inside of each tribe so they will pass on the north side of the rock. This is the p-point of the tribe that will move the least in the turn. Put the herds to the far, outside of the tribes and let them walk the full distance of the turn. Once the tribe is around the rock, they will continue to w-walk to the second turning point. The second turn back to the north will take place approximately one mile east of the rock. There will be a large banner to show where the tribes will make the second turn, just as they did in the first. The tribes will continue to keep one mile in distance between the them during and after each turn, moving together as a company." Moses paused a moment. "Once the last tribe has finished the second turn we will make camp." Joshua gave a nod of understanding.

Moses placed his hand on the drawing to show Joshua what he meant. Moses began to move around the drawing as he would have done when planning a battle in Egypt. He moved as a strategist planning an attack.

He stopped and turned to Joshua, "The ram's horn will be to signal the people, for starting, for stopping, as well as the sound of alarm. I will let you c-come up with the signals."

Joshua smiled back and said, "I've got a good idea for them." Joshua asked, "Just a question so I can answer those when they ask; if you were to go to the opposite end of the company and we just turned around, wouldn't that be easier?" He did his best to not sound as if he were questioning Moses or the Lord.

Moses smiled and said, "Yes. You will be asked this. The Lord has s-said we are to remain in the same order and to turn with the tribe of Judah in the front. I don't know why, and I don't question the Lord on this, b-but it is how He wants us to do it." He smiled at Joshua with a sense of Joshua understanding that Moses, himself, had questions he didn't understand.

Moses continued, "You will explain this plan to the tribal leaders in four groups of three each. You will call the meetings to b-be held in the middle tribe." The first group of three tribes are Judah, Issachar, and Zebulun. Moses pointed to Issachar's location on the picture and said, "The meeting will be held at the tent of Nethanel, the tribal leader of Issachar. The tribal leaders of Judah and Zebulun will come to his tent." The next three tribes of Reuben, Simeon, and Gad will meet at Simeon's tent. After them, Ephraim, Manasseh, and Benjamin. Then the final three tribes of Dan, Asher, and Naphtali will meet at Asher's tent." Moses looked at Joshua to make sure he understood. "Now concerning the tribe of Levi, because Aaron is traveling with me and is the leader of that tribe, they are dispersed throughout the company. They will receive instruction from the tribes they are traveling with. I want you to walk with the tribal leader of the first tribe to the meeting and send Acts to get the tribal leader of the third. It will be a four-to-five-mile walk-run for him." He smiled as he looked up from the drawing. "He is a fine young man and the Lord smiles on him."

Joshua smiled back and commented, "He's up for the challenge. He loves serving the Lord, you, and even me."

"He is more than a servant to b-both of us and especially you." Moses said with a cunning grin as he turned back to the drawing. "So that is how the meetings will be held."

Moses turned back to the drawing and combed his long white beard. He smiled and asked, "Did we c-cover everything?"

Joshua looked at the drawing and said softly, "The meetings, the order of the tribes, the spacing, the pivot point, the placing of the women, children and animals, the signals, runners, tribal leader banners…" He paused in thought and said, "I think we have."

"There will be things we have to take care of as we move. Some of those things you will have to take care of where you are." Moses said as he looked into the face of his servant and friend.

Joshua asked, "What do I tell them when they ask what we will do when we get to Pi Hahiroth?"

Moses looked off to the east and said, "I don't know all of what the Lord has planned, but He has told me a portion. I will share with you what I can Joshua, but some I must k-keep to myself for now." He smiled and said, "Now, I want you to take this parchment with you so that you can show the tribal leaders, just as I have shown you. I know that you c-can answer their questions, and I also know that you will do just as the Lord commands." Moses placed his hands on the shoulders of Joshua his servant and said, "Take courage and see what the Lord God will do."

Joshua looked into the face of the most-humble man on earth and could see a trust and faith in the Lord that he wanted in himself. Joshua replied, "It will be done just as you have instructed Moses."

He turned to go but, before he could, Moses gave him a hug and said as a father to a son, "I love you, my son."

Joshua answered, "As do I love you, servant of the Most-High God."

With that said, Joshua turned and found Acts waiting by the rock with the water and figs he was sent to get.

"I could see that you two were busy, so I waited out here and had a few figs." Acts said as he handed a fig to Joshua. "Do you know what we are to do?"

"Yes, I have the plan from Moses. Come on. I'll tell you on the way."

"Where are we going?" asked Acts.

"We are headed to the tent of Nethanel after you go to the tribe of Zebulun and escort Eliab back to Nethanel's tent for the meeting." Joshua answered.

Acts knew he would explain more as they walked. He thought for a moment and said, "That's about two and half miles from here and then about four miles back." Acts knew the distance between the tribes well, since he and Joshua had already passed through them going and coming back from the scouting trip. He looked up toward the direction they must travel and said, "I can do that!"

Joshua smiled at him and said, "Oh, I know you can. That's just what I told Moses." He paused and added, "I can think of three men who will *not* be happy with this decision."

Acts mimicked the other's expression. "Yes. I just wonder what they'll do when they hear."

"Korah will be the first to speak out against it," Joshua answered.

Acts kicked a rock. "Well, he'll just have to get over it. He's got three choices. He can go with the company, stay here, or go back to Egypt, but because he didn't get to give the order, he will swell up like a big toad."

Joshua laughed. "Whether he goes, stays, or swells up like a toad, he's the kind of man that can stir up trouble. We will have to be ready to react to him."

Acts looked at Joshua and thought out loud. "Going back through the tribes means one thing for sure…" Acts paused and cut his eyes to Joshua's face to gauge how closely Joshua was listening. "Klee's cooking."

Joshua grinned sheepishly. "You know, I was thinking almost the same thing."

CHAPTER 2

TROUBLE BREWING

As Joshua and Acts made their way through the first tribe of Judah, Joshua said to Acts, "I want to do something that may confuse you, but I think will work."

Acts looked back and said, "Ok. What is it?"

Joshua started, "Nahshon is a leader and is very proud of his family. He has a son, and I would like for *him* to escort you but…"

"But what?" Acts asked.

"But I would like for him to give the invitation to Eliab and Nethanel."

Acts looked back at Joshua, shrugged his shoulders and replied without hesitation, "Ok."

Joshua smiled and said, "I'm glad I won the argument."

They both laughed and Acts commented, "I'm here to serve not to argue."

Joshua smiled and said, "I wish they were all like you, little brother."

As they passed moved through the people, they could see they were happy and learning to enjoy something they never thought they would have, freedom.

Joshua and Acts approached Nahshon, the tribal leader of Judah holding up their right hands in greeting, they were rewarded with the same gesture from the older man. Nahshon smiled broadly. "Well Joshua, how is everything going?"

"It is going the way of freedom," Joshua answered.

Nahshon smiled. "Going the way of freedom. I like that."

Joshua quickly got down to business. "I would like to have a meeting at the tent of Nethanel by mid-morning, just before lunch. I am sending Acts ahead of us to accompany Eliab back, but I would like for your son to go with him and give the invitation to Nethanel and Eliab."

Nahshon smiled, turned, and waved for his middle son. He was a young man about the same size as Acts, lean, his musculature in the beginning stages of building strength with definition. "I would like for you to take the message of Joshua to the tribal leaders of Issachar and Zebulun. Let them know this is a meeting of importance and ask them to meet us at the tent of Nethanel. We will start the meeting when he arrives." The young man turned, and Nahshon put his arm on his son's shoulder and said softly, "You are given this honor because you are trustworthy. Walk with Eliab back to the meeting. Give them the message just as Joshua has given us. You are my son; represent us well, and remember I love you."

The young man matched the gaze of his father. "I will do as you have asked."

Nahshon turned to Acts and introduced him to his son, "This is my son, Salmon."

Acts put his hand out and replied, "It is good to meet you, Salmon. I am Acts. May I accompany you to bring Eliab back?"

Salmon gave him a strong handshake and answered, "It is good to meet you. Certainly, you may."

Joshua smiled and nodded toward Acts. "Go and be friends."

Because of the central location within the people, the meeting would be held in the tribe of Issachar. The sun was on its way to mid-morning by the time Acts and Salmon reached the tent of Nethanel.

On the way, Acts had learned that Salmon was the same age as he. His hands were calloused from work. Acts had watched Salmon's family and how his father treated him, and Acts had great respect for the young man already.

Salmon glanced at Acts. "You serve Joshua as Joshua serves Moses?"

"Yes," Acts replied. "The Lord has given me this honor. But in you, I see an honor that I have never known."

"What is that?" Salmon asked with a puzzled look on his face.

"You serve your father, who loves you and trusts you. My father wishes I had never been born." Bitterness chilled Acts' voice. "His heart is so dark with criticism he can't even follow Moses without complaining about his leadership."

Salmon felt compelled to keep asking about the young man who walked beside him. "Do you really think your father wishes you had never been born? Do you have other brothers and sisters? Does he wish they had never been born as well?"

Acts told him of his brothers and sisters. "No, he's never said that about them; only me. My mother died giving birth to me, so my sister, who is next to me in age, has been my mother, sister, and best friend. She is my family. The others have nothing to do with us; they have their own families and don't even come around at all."

Salmon's brows drew together in thought. "That is hard for me to understand. My family is so close, and we all work together taking care of, not only each other, but also those who are in our clan and tribe. It made serving under the hand of the Egyptians easier, in a way. Although many of our tribe died in Egypt, I think that is what brought us together."

Acts looked back at his tenderhearted companion and saw the confidence he possessed in making such bold statements about those whom he loved. Acts cleared his throat and said, "What did your family do in Egypt?"

"We were stone cutters. We made the columns that built some of the palaces and temples for the Egyptians. My father and uncles even served Pharaoh himself on one occasion. It was no honor; merely another thing to do as a slave."

"What did your family do with the stones?" asked Acts and then added, "My family only made bricks."

"In the palace by the pyramids, they made the pillars that supported the roof and porch. They worked two years building six pillars. I lost an uncle and a brother while there. In fact, my brother gave his life to save mine."

"Really? What happened?"

Salmon slowed the pace of their walk as he began to recall that day. "The pillar had five sections, and we were lifting the top section into place. I was on the ground with my brother holding one of the ropes that were around the section we were lifting. There were five other lines to it, and my father, cousins and uncles were holding them with the oxen pulling. It was during the spring rains, and my father tried to tell the overseer we needed time to make some new rope, because one of the lines we had was overused and had been wet for a couple of days. My father was afraid it had rotted on the inside. The overseer hit him with his whip and said, 'Use it anyway. We don't have time for you Hebrews to make more rope when you've got this one.'"

"With no choice, we used it. It was the line opposite my brother and me. The line broke, sending my uncle and cousin to the ground rolling on their backs near the team of oxen. The top section of the pillar came off, as if a horse had jerked it. I slipped, and my brother grabbed my hand and slung me out of the way, but he did not have time to move. We stood there gasping, in tears and disbelief. My father's heart was torn apart. I stood there, not knowing what to do…I couldn't think. All of a sudden, I felt the sharp pain of the whip."

Salmon's voice broke slightly, but he continued without giving in to it. "'Clean off that pillar and get it into place,' shouted the overseer. Down came the whip again. 'Get back to work! He's dead. I said get back to work!'"

It was the hate in Salmon's heart that allowed him to continue without crying. "They did not allow us to have a proper ceremony. They didn't even let us take the body. They just loaded what was left of my brother onto a cart and had some other Hebrews take him to the river and throw him to the crocodiles. It was the saddest day of my life."

Their pace slowed, almost to a stop. "My father came to me later, put his arm around me and told me, 'Your brother loved you very much, so much that he gave his life for you, and that is the greatest thing a man can do: give his life for another out of love. Now *we* must go on. I love you as I loved him, and I will always love you and be thankful to him for his sacrifice. Don't feel that I think this was your fault in any way. It is life, and life will go on. Now, let's get this job done, so we can go home.'"

Salmon swallowed hard. "I still don't know how he managed to say such kind words to me, but I will never forget them or the Egyptian who gave the order to have my brother thrown to the crocodiles." Salmon gritted his teeth. "Someday I will see him dead."

Acts placed a hand on Salmon's shoulder. "I don't know what it's like to lose a brother who died saving my life, but your brother was a great man, and I know our God saw that action and has rewarded him."

Salmon smiled. "Thank you, Acts."

The boys got their pace back up to speed and continued toward Nethanel's tent.

~

Joshua and Nahshon reclined in the older man's tent. "Who is this young man, Acts?" Nahshon asked.

Joshua told Nahshon that Acts was from his home tribe of Ephraim and that he had known Acts and his sister for several years. He also explained that Acts and Klee, his sister, were really their own family because their father hated Acts.

Nahshon frowned. "Why?"

"His mother died while giving birth to him and Klee has been his only mother figure, sister, and best friend in his life. Because Klee cared so for Acts, their father grew to hate her just as much."

Nahshon exhaled and leaned back. "I cannot even begin to understand a man like this. He should be seeing the blessing of what he has and loving them that much more."

Joshua nodded and took another sip from his water. "Their father began carousing with people of questionable character and soon he was completely consumed with the desire to just be like them. He didn't kick Klee and Acts out, because they actually took care of him."

Nahshon barked in surprise, "Even when they knew he hated them?" He leaned forward and grew quiet with intent. "Now I have a good picture of the character of Acts, and I'm glad he is with my son. They will become good friends—I can tell."

Joshua smiled. "Yes, they will be good for each other."

They finished their meal and began the journey to Nethanel's tent.

~

As Acts and Salmon approached Nethanel, they both raised a hand, and he returned the gesture with a smile.

"And who are you two young men?" Nethanel boomed.

Acts waited for a moment and then bumped Salmon with his shoulder. Salmon suddenly realized he was the one appointed to do the introductions and give the request. He cleared his throat. "I am Salmon, son of Nahshon, leader of Judah, and this is Acts, from the tribe of Ephraim. We have come with a message from Joshua, the servant of Moses, to ask if a meeting can be held at your tent this day before lunch with my father, Joshua, and Eliab?"

Nethanel studied the two young men. "What meeting is this?"

Salmon blinked and turned to Acts, not knowing how to answer. Acts stepped forward. "Joshua needs to give the instruction he received from Moses for the tribes in the coming days."

Nethanel looked back to Salmon. "I will have everything ready. Is there anything else?"

Salmon glanced quickly to Acts before answering, and Acts shook his head. "No, that's about it." A moment passed before Salmon shifted his weight and awkwardly announced the need for their departure. "Well, we should continue. We must escort Eliab to your tent."

Acts whispered to Salmon as he turned to leave, "Say, 'Thank you.'"

Salmon spun around. "Oh and thank you very much."

Nethanel smiled at Salmon. "It's my honor."

Once away from the tent, Salmon breathed deeply in relief. "Thanks for doing that. I hadn't stopped to think about how to present the reason for the meeting. How did you know what to say?"

Acts shrugged. "I wouldn't have known what to say if Joshua hadn't taught me."

Even under the covering of the cloud, the mid-morning heat hung heavy in the air when they arrived at the tent of Eliab. Salmon possessed more confidence this time because of what Acts had shared with him. Eliab was a very likeable man, and he agreed to walk back with them to the meeting. Salmon's presentation was very mannered, and it left an impression on Eliab.

"You must have great potential if you serve with Joshua," the older man commented.

Salmon smiled ruefully. "I don't serve with Joshua; Acts does. I was sent by my father at Joshua's request."

"Well, I still stand by what I said," Eliab replied. "You have great potential, Salmon."

Salmon stood a little taller.

~

Joshua and Nahshon arrived at Nethanel's tent only a few minutes before Acts, Salmon, and Eliab.

After the exchanging of greetings, Nethanel gestured for all of them to sit and take some of the refreshments he had prepared. Once everyone was comfortable, Joshua began to speak. Acts watched and listened to his mentor explain the command and how to accomplish the beginning of such a huge undertaking. Acts admired Joshua for his clarity of thought and ability to put this plan in such logical and easy-to-understand terms and descriptions. Turning a few million people in the opposite direction was no small task. Acts marveled at the mere thought of it, and he wondered how they were going to prevent panic and confusion during the movement.

Joshua spoke with authority, with a style that caught the attention of the leaders. Joshua's words flowed with wisdom beyond his years.

"Moses has received word from the Lord God that we are to turn back and camp at Pi Hahiroth."

There was an immediate feeling of objection, but Joshua continued.

"I know it is back in the direction of Egypt, but we serve a God who has brought us out of slavery and is still leading us through Moses. Moses has told me not to trust in what I see, and to understand obedience is what our God demands. We serve the only true God, and He has shown that He is faithful. Did He not keep the Destroyer from the House of Jacob?" Joshua referred to the Hebrews as the House of Jacob to stir their feelings of brotherhood, since they all descended from the family of Jacob, Abraham's grandson. It bound the company together as one entity instead of twelve different tribes.

Joshua could see the concern and questions on the faces of those present and paused for a moment to allow the emotions in the tent to condense. "The order of the tribes is to remain the same as it was in leaving Egypt." Joshua pulled out a piece of parchment and began to explain how the process would be carried out just as Moses had explained to him.

He stopped again to let the men study the picture and his description. He paused to make sure that each tribal leader understood.

"I would also like for you to appoint skilled fighting men, for protection, to be posted within the boundaries on the outermost part of each tribe. I will give the signals of the rams' horn we have used since leaving Egypt. They will stay the same with the exception of the signal to turn for the tribe that is at the rock. The signal for battle will only be given should a tribe come under attack and from that sound, other tribes will react in the direction of that signal. Message runners will be very important and will carry a flag with them at all times so other runners can identify them. The entire company will continue keeping about one mile between each tribe until Moses gives the order to stop. Keep watch on the men with flags at the boundaries and maintain the integrity of the tribe as we move. Once the last tribe has made the second turn we are to camp for a short while. If any problems arise, I will take them to Moses, and he will go to the Lord for the answer."

As he looked into the faces of the wise men before him, he found a peace that the plan would work.

"We will begin to turn when Acts and I have gone through the rest of the company. When we travel back through this way, you will know the time is near. The rest the Lord has given us here at Etham has been good for everyone. Be patient with each other and with yourselves." He stopped, looking each leader in the eyes. "Have I made the plan clear?" Each smiled and nodded, showing they understood.

Eliab of the tribe of Zebulun spoke. "I can hardly believe we've managed to stay in a line this far anyway."

That brought some laughter and Joshua put his hand out for Acts to depart, allowing Salmon to return with Nahshon. Lifting Acts to his feet, Joshua said, "Well, my friend, let's see if the others take it so well."

~

Joshua rolled up the parchment as Acts complimented him when they were walking away from the meeting. He told Joshua, "You really explained that well."

"Moses is a master planner. I know Nahshon, Eliab, and Nethanel are dedicated men and will do as Moses has said."

Acts asked Joshua, "I would like to ask that Salmon join us in this mission through the tribes—if you see that it would be good."

Joshua thought for a moment. "Do you see the type of character in him needed to do as Moses has been commanded?"

Acts paused to consider his young friend, and he looked into the eyes of his captain and replied, "He is strong and loves his father and Moses. His character is one I would want to have."

"Then I guess I should go back and ask Nahshon for his permission."

As Joshua turned to go speak with the older leader, Acts spoke in his heart, *'Lord, thank you for bringing a friend to me that is my age.'*

Acts looked up to see Nahshon hugging Salmon and then Salmon turning to walk back with Joshua. As Acts fell into step with Joshua, he grinned at Salmon. "So, I take it you're in with us?"

"Until the mission is accomplished," Salmon replied with a smile.

Acts stated, "If we rest on the far side of the tribe of Gad, we could have Klee make us some of her stew."

"Will your father be around? Maybe you won't have to see him?" Salmon asked.

Acts stared at the ground. "Yes. He will be there."

Salmon felt the disappointment in Acts' heart, and he ached for his new friend.

Joshua nodded, placing his hand on Acts' shoulder. "I think eating with your sister would be a great idea!" He took another look at Acts' face and saw the look of disappointment had changed to one of scheming. "Now don't get any big ideas, my friend."

"Oh, I wasn't," Acts said quickly as he started walking to the next tribe, hiding his grin from his companion. "I wasn't!" he insisted at Joshua's arched eyebrow.

Salmon looked blankly from Acts to Joshua. "What big idea?"

Acts and Joshua just laughed.

Salmon replied. "What?"

Joshua stopped, still chuckling at Salmon's obliviousness, and said, "We can make it to the tent of Elizur, the tribal leader of Reuben by mid-afternoon. You two can get word of the meeting to Shelumiel as you pass through; get Eliasaph, and escort him back to the meeting. We will only be a few miles from Klee. We can easily make it to her, by supper."

The two boys looked at Joshua with surprise. He looked back at them and said, "You can do it. It is only about five to six miles to the tent of Eliasaph. You can make it back to Simeon, by mid-afternoon."

They understood the timing and nothing else was said about the run. The three started a slow run to the tribe of Reuben and then picked up the pace. It would be a few miles to the tent of the Elizur, taking short rests and making sure to drink plenty of water.

It was early afternoon, when Joshua, Acts, and Salmon approached the tribe of Reuben and found Elizur, the tribal leader. He was a dedicated man and a good leader. He led by example, and the effects were evident throughout his entire group.

"Hoshea—I mean, Joshua. I'm sorry, my friend. I keep trying to remember your new name, but I've known you a long time as Hoshea. It will take me a while to get used to 'Joshua.'"

Joshua smiled. "Elizur, it's good to see you. How is your wife and children?"

"Since we have left Egypt, my wife sings constantly. The boys are bewildered by her behavior, saying they've never seen her this way, but then, none of us have ever been this happy. It's hard for me to explain when I am experiencing freedom for the first time, too. The girls are starting to learn some of the songs their mother sings, but Miriam and my wife keep coming up with more to praise our God. To think of where we are and how we arrived here is so miraculous it is almost too much for me to take in."

He paused, a faraway look settling on his face. When he spoke again, it was with quiet intensity. "My entire family, other than my wife and children, died at the hands of the Egyptians in slavery. And now, being free only makes me want to serve God that much more."

He smiled at Joshua. "Speaking of serving; how is Moses? I've not been able to talk with him since our last meeting."

"Moses is fine," replied Joshua. "He has a message for all the tribes from the Lord. Will you come with me to the tribe of Simeon to meet with Shelumiel and Eliasaph in order for me to give you the instructions?"

Elizur nodded. "When do we leave?"

Joshua looked toward the two teenagers behind him. "Soon. I am sending Acts and Salmon ahead to ask Shelumiel to get things ready. They will go to Gad and ask Eliasaph to come and escort him back."

The two young men bid their farewells, leaving Elizur and Joshua to have good fellowship and get caught up on family news.

~

A short time passed before they came to Shelumiel, the leader of the tribe of Simeon. A very matter-of-fact kind of man, he understood that God had chosen Moses to free them from bondage. Acts and Salmon both raised a hand in honor approaching Shelumiel's tent and the gesture was returned. Salmon gave the request for the meeting at his tent, and then listed the others to be in attendance. Shelumiel studied this young man and, as he nodded in agreement, said, "My tent is always open to Joshua and the men who serve with him."

Salmon replied, "We should have no problem being back by midday or a little after."

"Very well," Shelumiel replied. "Be on your guard with those who belong to the tribe of Levi who are traveling with the tribe of Gad. Some have been filtering through several of the tribes and causing trouble." He turned around and retrieved a small loaf of unleavened bread and gave it to Salmon. "This will tell Eliasaph that the meeting is important and will show, you have a specific person this bread is intended."

Shelumiel held Salmon's gaze as he continued. "Sometimes people think more highly of themselves than they should. But it will be alright. You go and fulfill what Joshua has sent you to do. We will be here, and upon your arrival, we will begin the meeting."

The boys affirmed in unison and turned to start a slow-paced run to the tribe of Gad.

Acts took a deep breath. "I don't know what's happening, but I guess we'll find out soon enough."

Salmon pondered the possible scenarios before deciding that it did not matter what he imagined or prepared for; it would always be different. Changing the subject, he asked Acts what he thought of all the things the Lord did getting them out of Egypt.

It was not long before their focus was back on the Lord.

CHAPTER 3

CHALLENGE

Acts and Salmon talked of how it felt to be free and the wonder they both felt in witnessing the Lord God create such powerful plagues. They both were bursting with questions about where they would go and what kind of land God was taking them to. They spoke of the stories of Joseph and what little was known of Jacob. During their conversation, they had not noticed how far they had traveled into the tribe of Gad.

Acts stopped and looked around. "I don't have any idea where Eliasaph's tent would be." They began searching for something to signify the leader's dwelling, and they noticed a man standing in front of a tent several yards away. Thinking that he might be able to point them in the right direction, they approached him, holding up a hand in greeting. But no hand rose in return.

Acts allowed Salmon to introduce them. "I am Salmon, son of Nahshon of the tribe of Judah, and this is Acts of the tribe of Ephraim. We come to give a message from Joshua to Eliasaph."

"What message?" The man snapped.

To Acts' surprise, Salmon showed no reaction to the abrupt retort. "Joshua needs to pass along instructions which Moses received from the Lord." Salmon's reply was calm and polite.

Acts stood slightly behind Salmon, but suddenly he felt urged to move up beside his friend. With Acts' silent reinforcement, Salmon continued. "There will be a meeting at the tent of Shelumiel for Elizur, Shelumiel and Eliasaph in order for Joshua to—"

"*I* am the leader of the tribe of Levi while Aaron is with Moses!" spat the man.

Salmon replied. "I'm sorry, I didn't know. Since the tribe of Levi are dispersed throughout the company, they will get instruction with the tribal leaders they are traveling with."

"Who are you?" Acts demanded, his voice strong and without fear.

The man puffed up. "I am Korah, the cousin of both Aaron and Moses." He turned to stare at Acts. "And what did *you* say your name was again, *boy?*"

Acts squared off his shoulders to the man and looked down into his eyes. "I am Acts, the servant of Joshua, the servant of Moses."

Korah looked up into the eyes of this young teenager and saw a bold and strong spirit. Even though Acts' physique still lacked mature development, promise bunched in his muscles, and his height had reached the point of manly respect, being at least four inches taller than Korah. Acts' deep blue eyes, rare for a Hebrew, stayed fixed and steady on the older man's face. Korah's brow furrowed, and with a snarl in his lips, he backed down for the moment.

Salmon looked from Korah to Acts, swallowed and continued. "We are to take this bread to Eliasaph and ask him to walk back with us."

Korah never took his eyes off Acts. Acts' gaze did not shift from eye to eye but simply looked with great intensity into Korah's left eye. Korah faltered slightly under Acts' strong stare. He cleared his throat gruffly. "I will go tell Eliasaph about the meeting." He held out his hands to take the bread from Salmon, but Salmon pulled the bread back to himself. "I am to give this bread to Eliasaph only."

"Give it to me, boy, and I will take it to him," Korah snapped.

"I'm sorry, but I cannot," Salmon replied, sounding calmer than he really felt.

Infuriated, Korah took a step toward Salmon, but Salmon stood his ground, keeping the bread close to his chest. Korah looked at the young man and then at Acts, and Korah decided this was not the time, because he was alone with no support.

"We will be walking with Eliasaph if you wish to follow," Acts stated.

Korah winced at his last word. "I will be there," he growled, "and I am going to bring two others who share an interest in this meeting also. You'd better wait on starting the meeting until we get there, boy."

Acts refused to be intimidated. "The meeting will start when we arrive with Eliasaph, whether you are in attendance, or not."

Salmon, seeing his opportunity to leave, walked around Korah. Acts followed but Korah brushed his arm as he passed, giving a silent message. Acts turned to look Korah in the eyes one more time, studying the man's build and how he held his hands and his stance. It gave a silent message that both understood.

They finally found Eliasaph's tent. As they approached, Salmon held up his hand, and the tribal leader returned the kind gesture. Salmon gave him the bread and asked him to walk with them back to the meeting.

"Certainly," the man answered as he reached for his staff. "How's that sister of yours, Acts?"

Salmon looked with surprise back to Acts.

"She's very caught up in thinking of a certain individual these days," Acts replied, unable to stop the grin from flowering on his face.

Eliasaph laughed. "Then I guess Joshua has been a bit too busy to stop by much lately?"

"Yes, sir, but we are hoping to see her this evening." Acts looked to Salmon. "My sister knows Eliasaph's daughters and has spent a lot of time with them."

Salmon read in his friend's voice and heart that their time spent together was to escape Uebel, Act's father.

There was a moment of silence before Eliasaph asked dryly, "Well, did you both have the opportunity to meet Korah?"

Acts glanced over at Salmon, paused, and told Eliasaph all that was said. Acts scrunched up his face as he gave expression to his feelings without being rude. "He is a little annoying."

The others looked at him.

Acts smiled sheepishly. "Well, maybe not just a little."

~

Meanwhile, Joshua had time to visit with his friend Elizur, who brought up the "new feeling of freedom" that seemed good and yet uncertain at the same time.

He leaned back on his pillow, and looking at Joshua, "I know that in our lifetime, we have never known anything but slavery; nothing gained. I also know that the Lord God showed His mighty power to not only the Egyptians, but to us as a nation during the plagues. I remember the cries laid before this God we know very little about— cries to be free, to see the fulfillment of stories that have been told for generations. Now that I…that *we* are free, I don't really know how to feel or what to say. What do I do with the feelings I'm so used to having as a slave? I have felt them for so long, had them literally *whipped* into me, and I can't just turn them off. Yet I know this is the time for change. How *do* I change?" He looked deep into Joshua's eyes to see if his attempt to explain part of his heart had been successful.

Joshua rubbed his face and then leaned over to grab a piece of bread and dip it in some grape juice. He sighed. "I have been dealing with the same thoughts. I have felt such hate for most Egyptians all my life and now…those feelings have no one to hate. In seeing the power of God, the God that some of us have worshiped in secret in our homes, it sometimes terrifies me to think what would happen next if the nation were to turn their back on Him out in this wilderness."

"Elizur, we saw ten plagues that brought the most powerful nation in the world to its knees, yet for nine of them the king's heart remained like stone. Passover was the most terrifying thing I have ever experienced. Four days I took care of that little lamb. I wanted it to be so perfect for the Lord and when it came time to kill it… to sacrifice it so I would be spared and passed over…I found in my heart an ache I had never known before. I loved that lamb, but our God required its blood."

"I know what you mean, Joshua," Elizur said quietly, pausing the journey of a piece of bread to his mouth. "Never have I seen so much blood for it to flow in the streets by my house. This God we serve, I know so little about him. I have only been told the stories and hoped in my heart He was real and did indeed care for me." Elizur looked off into the distance, the piece of bread forgotten and dropped back into the dish.

Joshua posed a question, one that seemed to have wisdom far beyond his years. "Why do you think there were no bones allowed to be broken in the sacrificed animals? Do you think there will be a perfect sacrifice someday?"

Elizur turned to look at Joshua. He studied his face and found the question puzzling; "A perfect sacrifice?" Elizur repeated, shaking his head. "How could there be a *Perfect Sacrifice*? My friend, I still have trouble just trying to understand what I have seen. The thought that death passed over our houses because it saw the blood of a sacrifice on its doorframes was too much for me to understand. Death—the Destroyer—lingered outside my door. I was terrified. I sat with my staff in hand, bags packed the whole time. I ate the meat and those awful bitter herbs, wondering what would happen next in my life. My family was so frightened not a word of conversation was spoken the entire night."

He paused to sip some water and then continued softly, "I kept thinking, 'What if my sacrifice was not good enough?'" The question floated through Joshua's mind several times. He stopped to ponder it. Elizur continued, "What if I had prepared it the wrong way, or if I had something in my life, something hidden the Destroyer would find that could give him a way into my home… to be able to kill my oldest son?"

Joshua put his hand on his friend's shoulder and shook him a little. "But we made it! The Lord did just as Moses said he would."

"Yes, my friend, yes!" Elizur breathed deeply. "It is hard to think that Israel and Egypt once lived in harmony. The Pharaoh who knew Joseph loved him very much. He surely was his closest friend."

"Oh, I agree," said Joshua, getting excited as he continued. "The dreams and their interpretations, the nerve-wracking wait to see if what was predicted came to pass—"

"—and the forgiveness that Joseph had for his brothers and the plan to take care of them," Elizur continued. "What an awesome thought, to be forgiven for such wrong." The question that Joshua had proposed floated back through' Elizur's mind, *'Could there be a perfect sacrifice to forgive all sin?'*

Silence controlled the moment briefly, and Elizur continued. "But what Joseph's brothers did to him does not compare with what the Egyptians put on us. The labor, the pain…" He paused to keep back the tears.

"The death," Joshua finished.

"Yes! The death."

After a moment, Joshua decided to change the subject. "Our two young messengers should be escorting Eliasaph back to us by now."

Elizur, seeing Joshua's heart trying to ease his own, flowed with the change of tone. "I think it's about time for us to start to Shelumiel's tent and see if they beat us there."

~

About the same time Elizur reached for his staff to walk with Joshua; Acts and Salmon were ready to begin their trek with Eliasaph. Falling to one knee, Acts covered his right ear. Salmon and Eliasaph tried to catch him, but he fell hard to the ground and rolled on his left side. His breathing almost stopped.

Salmon glanced to Eliasaph in complete fear. "Is he dead?"

Eliasaph checked the boy's body. "No, he's still breathing, even though it is shallow and slow."

He leaned down and gently shook Acts. The young man tried to open his eyes for his elder, but his body would not respond, and the image of his friends morphed into visions of danger as his consciousness slipped into another dream.

Colors swirled in his mind, faces appearing and then fading away. Acts' body flinched as the pictures fought through his mind. The pillar of cloud that led the company by day floated to the forefront of the barrage of images, only to be forced out later and replaced by a vision of the pillar of fire. Egyptians whipped their horses in chase. He could see the muscles of the horses working and their run seemed to be so slow to his eye. He could see the dust and rocks individually as they were kicked up by the hooves of the great animals.

Acts awoke to the feel of cool water pouring over his forehead and through his hair. His vision stayed blurry at first, and then the sound of voices pierced through the fog. He heard a deep, older voice calling to him. "Acts! *Acts!* Are you alright?"

Acts blinked and nodded his head slightly. He started to rise, but Eliasaph, who had voiced the question, laid his hand on Acts' shoulder and pushed him back down. "Hold on. Just lay back for a moment, Acts. You're still a bit too confused to get up."

Acts closed his eyes again. "How long?"

"Only a minute or so," Eliasaph replied.

Salmon began rattling off questions, his nervous energy rushing out in a barrage of words. "Are you alright? You scared me to death, Acts! Did you get too hot? Do you need to eat or get some sleep? Do you—"

Acts held up his hand, grimacing. "I'm fine, Salmon. Calm down. No, I didn't get too hot, and yes, I am hungry."

Eliasaph sent two young women to bring some bread and water. They ran off, and Eliasaph helped Acts sit up. "Can you stand?"

"I believe so," Acts replied. Eliasaph and Salmon helped Acts into the tent.

His word supply exhausted, Salmon now sat still and quiet, his face white. He seemed to have more trouble recovering from the episode than Acts. Acts grasped Eliasaph's arm. "Thank you for your kindness." He paused; his face thoughtful. "That happens sometimes, and I don't think Korah would have been so caring."

Eliasaph chuckled. "I must agree." Becoming more serious he asked, "Do you know why this happens to you?"

"No." Acts answered, rubbing his face. "But I do have some pretty colorful dreams."

Eliasaph leaned back against a cushion and changed the subject. "So, this meeting must be pretty important."

Acts looked to Salmon, a gesture to let Salmon know that *he* was supposed to answer Eliasaph. Salmon's eyes opened wide, and he stammered, "Oh! Joshua has instructions from Moses for the tribes concerning the coming days."

Eliasaph smiled at Salmon. "I don't think we were officially introduced."

Salmon, still shaken over Acts' episode, took a moment before answering. "I am Salmon, the son of Nahshon of the tribe of Judah," he pointed to his friend, "and this is Acts."

Acts looked at Eliasaph and then back at Salmon. "He knows me, Salmon. He was asking who your dad is and to what tribe you belong." Acts turned to Eliasaph and grinned. "He usually doesn't have this much trouble talking."

That brought a laugh, and everyone relaxed.

About that time, the two young ladies Eliasaph had sent for food returned and served the young men. Acts recognized them and smiled. But he suddenly remembered that he had probably fainted in front of them, and his face burned with embarrassment.

Janue spoke first. "Are you feeling better, Acts? Do you hurt anywhere?"

"I…uhm…yes, thank you…and no, I don't hurt." His eyes caught Salmon's, and his friend smirked at him, silently saying, "Now look who's having trouble talking."

Wanting to remove the full attention from himself, Acts gestured toward Salmon. "This is my friend, Salmon. I have been sent to assist him on his mission."

"A *mission?*" Shade repeated excitedly. "You must be someone of importance then!" She smiled at Salmon.

Eliasaph could see the "teenage moment" becoming a bit thick. "Thank you, girls," he said, dismissing them. "That will be enough. These boys can't stay long. They must escort me to a meeting, right, boys?"

"Yes, sir!" they hurriedly answered.

"Just as soon as we finish eating," Acts added.

When the food had disappeared from the serving dishes, the boys thanked Eliasaph's wife and the girls who had served them. Acts asked Janue, "Do you think you and Shade will be seeing Klee soon?"

The two girls looked at their father for the answer, and with the nod of his head Janue answered, "Yes!"

Acts lowered his voice slightly. "Will you ask her to fix some of her stew for Joshua and me?" Salmon elbowed Acts in the side and Acts immediately added, "And for Salmon?" The young ladies nodded and walked off, smiling at the two young men who watched with such open, adolescent admiration.

Eliasaph shook his head and laughed. He slapped Salmon on his back and helped Acts to his feet. "Okay, boys. Let's get going."

As they left the tent area, Salmon gently pushed Acts and said, "Mission? We're on a *mission?*"

Acts shrugged. "Well, it sounded better than 'messenger boys.'"

"'You must be someone of importance,'" Salmon said in a high-pitched voice. "I didn't know what to say. In fact, I felt like an idiot."

"Well, you certainly looked like one," Acts teased.

Salmon blushed and playfully shoved Acts over a few feet. "Whatever. You weren't all that articulately blessed, either."

Eliasaph laughed at the boys' banter and urged them to pick up the pace.

The sun was high in the deep-blue sky above the pillar of cloud, and the boys were surprised to find they had a hard time keeping up with Eliasaph, instead of the other way around. It looked like they would make it in time to start the meeting as planned.

Eliasaph slowed the boys down to caution them as they drew nearer to the encampment. "Korah, Dathan, and Abiram are three men looking to be 'great' at any cost. They care nothing for Moses, and they don't listen to anyone but their own selfish hearts. They are all dangerous and reckless. Watch every move they make and be on your guard always." The boys exchanged glances and Acts nodded toward Eliasaph. "You can count on that."

As Eliasaph, Salmon, and Acts approached the area where they had first met Korah, they could see Korah standing with Dathan, Abiram, and the sons of Aaron, Nadab and Abihu, along with several other men. They watched the boys as Eliasaph walk toward them. They seem to spread out to give Korah room to show that *he* was the acting leader. As before, Salmon and Acts raised their hands in greeting and, as before, no one raised a hand in return. The three men could sense instability in the coming moment, and Eliasaph was the first to speak, even though the greeting was difficult. "Greetings, men of Levi."

Korah spoke first. "We've been talking this meeting over, and Dathan, Abiram, and I think it would be best if you and the other tribal leaders let me do all the talking with Joshua. We need to keep the 'best interest' of *our* tribes in focus. There are a number of people to keep in mind, and we want the best for them."

Eliasaph, as well as Salmon and Acts, knew this was a pile of camel dung. The only *interests* they kept in mind were their own. They were hungry for followers and would say anything to ensure such a gathering. Acts started to speak, "You can think you wan—"

"I think the meeting," interrupted Eliasaph, "would be the best time to decide such a matter, don't you?" He looked around at the other men standing there. As each one heard the wisdom of Eliasaph, they finally shook their heads in agreement, igniting anger in Korah.

"*What?* You men are listening to an old man who thinks in old ways! We need new blood in the leadership for the future of the people of Israel, and listening to *old* men is not the way to lead the people into victory in battle with the Philistines!"

It was at this point Acts could not keep silent. "And what if the Lord God has given Moses different instructions?"

"Moses is a shepherd, not a general of Pharaoh's army anymore." Korah spat. "Yes, he got us out of Egypt, but now we need a leader who knows where to go and what to do."

"And you have the name of this leader?" Acts said with a fair amount of anger.

"Yes! Me!"

Acts knew Korah would make Dathan and Abiram part of his staff of leadership, and they would then have the recognition they desired in their hearts, something akin to being *worshiped*.

Acts continued, not bothering to check his anger. "And *you* have this experience in battle? A man who has been a slave all of his life; doing just as he was told, leading no one?"

This catalyzed Korah's anger to action. He lunged toward Acts and threw his fist toward Acts' jaw. When Korah's arm had fully extended, Acts dodged the punch and stepped into Korah's body with his back, grabbing Korah's arm with both hands. Acts bent slightly over and pulled Korah over his shoulder, causing Korah to land on his back in front of Acts. All the air in Korah rushed out with great force. Acts stepped back, ready for another attacker to advance, but while Acts was busy throwing Korah around, Salmon had stepped up beside Acts in a stance ready for combat.

No one else moved. In fact, no one expected it would go this far so soon. Dathan stepped back with the other men, surprised at the sudden outburst between their leader and a teenager.

Korah struggled to his feet, and after regaining his balance and his second wind, rushed toward Acts. As Korah pulled back to swing at Acts, Acts thrust his fist up into Korah's throat, sending him backward, the beaten man grasping his throat in an attempt to pull air into his lungs and swallow. Acts moved forward and pushed on Korah's forehead, sending him to the ground hard on his seat. This sent a jolt up his back to his head. Acts and Salmon moved forward in one fluid movement, and now the two stood back-to-back with

Eliasaph in the middle of them. No one moved, and the only sound was Korah gasping for air.

Eliasaph finally broke the silence. He smoothed his robes and tightened his grip on his staff. "Well, then, since we have that settled, we will be going. The meeting begins when I arrive, and we will begin whether you are present or not. The information will be given to the other tribes, and it will be followed, since Moses is the man, the Lord God has placed in position to lead the company of Israel. Do as you think best, though I advise you to take these last few minutes into consideration." He added, "And I would also consider that Moses is the one the Lord called."

Salmon and Acts both backed away from the group, Eliasaph behind them for his protection. Abiram spoke. "Acts, you will pay for this."

Acts straightened to his full height and replied, "I stand as the servant of Joshua, the servant of Moses, and I answer to those two men as I answer to the Lord God, who speaks through them. You can take your case before Moses and the Lord, and there, wisdom will decide what I will pay!" Acts turned with his companions in the direction of the tribe of Simeon.

Salmon and Eliasaph kept stealing glances at Acts as they walked. When they were some distance away from the scene, Acts looked back at them and blurted, "What?"

Eliasaph spoke quietly. "I have never seen such a thing."

"Nor have I," added Salmon.

Acts felt his face turn red. "It was nothing, really. It kind of just came to me." He felt uncomfortable with the look of amazement on Salmon's face and thoughtfulness on Eliasaph's. "Joshua taught me." He admitted.

The other two shook their heads. "Well, you make a very fine student," Eliasaph complimented. "Although," he added, looking meaningfully at Acts, "you might want to keep working on your temper."

Acts nodded ruefully. "Yes, sir."

"Do you think Joshua, or you could teach me that?" Salmon asked hopefully.

Acts' countenance lifted considerably. "I would be glad to, my friend."

Eliasaph chuckled. "I'm too old for it, but it certainly looked like fun."

~

It was late afternoon when the trio arrived at the tribe of Simeon, and they came upon Shelumiel's tent. They had made better time than expected.

Shelumiel welcomed the boys as they walked up to the men, and he greeted Eliasaph. "It is good to see you, Eliasaph. You're looking good for a man your age."

Eliasaph laughed. "That's good, considering we are the same age."

Joshua turned to his two young warriors. "How did it go?"

Salmon glanced at Acts before answering. "Pretty smooth... I guess?" Salmon replied hesitantly.

Joshua arched an eyebrow. "What do you mean, 'pretty smooth?'"

Salmon looked at Acts and Acts looked at Joshua before saying, "We had a...situation arise with Korah, Dathan, and Abiram."

Joshua's silence prompted Acts to continue. "He informed us of his position, and since there was no one else to ask, we told him of the meeting, but we had to go around him to give Eliasaph the bread."

Joshua looked at Acts and asked, "What bread?"

Shelumiel replied, "I gave them a small loaf of bread for them to present to Eliasaph. I knew if they met with Korah, he would want to be in control of telling Eliasaph about the meeting in his own way. The bread just presented a way of getting around Korah.

Joshua turned back to Acts and Salmon and asked, "Did it work?"

"Yes, sir." They both answered.

Joshua studied the boys, knowing there was more than they were telling. "So, what was the situation?"

As Acts began to recount the events that had taken place with Korah, Joshua listened intently, noting the uncomfortable sound in the boy's voice as he described the fight between him and Korah. Joshua was very aware of Acts watching him for his reactions to his story, and that told him Acts was greatly concerned with what he thought of him. Acts finished, standing silently and nervously in the center of the tent. Joshua glanced at Eliasaph, and Eliasaph nodded his head slightly. Satisfied with this confirmation and support of the story, Joshua stood and placed a hand on Acts' shoulder. "Well done."

Acts relief was obvious, and he gave a glance to Salmon and then to Eliasaph with a "thank you" in his smile.

Elizur asked, "Who will be representing the Levites?"

Eliasaph answered, "Korah."

There was a pause and as Eliasaph said, "I told them, when I arrive the meeting would begin, with or without their presence."

"What did Korah say?" Joshua asked.

Eliasaph laughed and answered, "Nothing after Acts popped him in the throat. He was more preoccupied with breathing."

Joshua looked at Eliasaph and could not keep from laughing with him. He pictured it in his mind. And the more he thought about it, the more he laughed, and soon all of them were laughing. When they finally calmed down, Shelumiel motioned for everyone to be seated for some refreshments. The conversation began to turn back to the reason of the meeting, and as Joshua began to speak, he looked up and saw Korah, Dathan, and Abiram approaching the tent. He stood to greet them but did not raise his hand. Joshua's face was passive and inscrutable—no smile, no indication of emotion. He simply offered his hand in a gesture as to where they were to sit. They sat down without a word. Korah's glare lingered on Acts as Joshua began by spreading out the parchment for everyone to see.

"Moses, the servant of the Lord, has been given instructions as to what the entire company of Israel is to do next," Joshua announced. "We are to turn back to Pi Hahiroth between Migdol and the Red Sea."

Questions immediately started flying around the tent. Joshua raised his hand to quiet the barrage. "Allow me to relay all the instructions, and *then* we will discuss what you do not understand." That brought the meeting back to order. "At the sound of the ram's horn from my position on the rock…" the instructions came as clearly as he had given the first time. Coming to the end of the instructions, Joshua stated, "The water carts are to be dispersed so each clan will only have to walk a short distance for water. The water level is dropping, and we need to make it last until the next oasis."

"Oh?" interjected Abiram, his face fashioned into mock concern. "And where would that be?"

Joshua refused to give in to frustration. "We will reach the tributaries that flow into the sea. There we will fill the carts. I must travel to the rear guard to give this report and the instructions you have heard. Acts and Salmon will serve with me. As we pass through your camps once again, you will know the time to turn will be soon."

As expected, Korah spoke next, but his voice was quiet and raspy—a result of the blow from Acts. "I think it would be more easily accomplished if the company simply turned around and went in reverse order and forgot this turning around business."

"These are the instructions given Moses the servant of the Lord Most High and we will follow them to the letter," Joshua interrupted. "Our God demands obedience and does not need our ideas on what we 'think' might be easiest. He is a mysterious God, but He is the One who delivered us from the hand of the Egyptians, and" Joshua leaned toward Korah, "it is at *His* command that we turn back and stay in the order He gave us when we left Egypt."

Joshua answered with authority, and it demanded respect. Korah was not about to stand and bristle against him. He knew well the warrior reputation Joshua carried. It was Joshua who helped train and exercise some of the elite forces of the Pharaoh, for even though they despised the Hebrews, they respected those with fighting ability. And rather than waste their ability on labor, that talent was cultivated so that Egypt benefited, as well as the families of those who trained with the Egyptians. The return was not much, but it was a small benefit the Egyptians gave back to them.

Joshua stepped back and looked at each of the other tribal leaders, silently asking for questions. No one said anything. Joshua rolled the parchment and stated. "Acts, Salmon, and I will be on our way. We must try and get back to the front as soon as possible. We will pass by each of your tribes on the way back through. You will know when to start at the sound of the ram's horn. Be patient with each other and with yourselves. God has a wonderful plan for us, and we must trust Him and Moses, His servant."

As Joshua pulled Acts and Salmon to their feet, he said, "The sun is beginning to set; we should be on our way."

When they were away from the tent and the other men, Salmon looked over at Joshua and commented, "That went well. Don't you think?"

Acts could not keep from laughing, and the levity was much appreciated.

The three left Shelumiel's tent at a slow pace to reach the far side of Gad. They were not in a hurry. As the sun was falling in the western sky, the pillar of cloud diminished, and the Lord God showed His presence with His people through the pillar of fire. The light shone just bright enough for them to see, but it still allowed the stars to shine.

As the three settled in for the night, Salmon added, "I am looking forward to meeting Klee in the morning."

CHAPTER 4

THE BUILDING OF A FAMILY

Up early, before the sun began to rise the next morning, the three were rested and excited. For Joshua and Acts the run to their home tribe was quick. As they approached the tent, they found Klee up and she met them, giving Acts a hug and then Joshua.

Acts asked, "Are you up early because of our father?"

She nodded and told him, "He came in early this morning after spending time with Korah and his goons." Acts understood and let the conversation change. He turned and gestured to Salmon. "Klee, this is Salmon of the tribe of Judah. His father is Nahshon, the tribal leader, and he has joined us."

Salmon stood with his mouth open at the sight of this beautiful woman. He could hardly believe she was Acts' sister. Her blue eyes were the same as Acts. Acts elbowed him fairly hard, and Salmon realized his stupor and sputtered, "I…uh…I sure am glad to meet you, Klee."

She laughed like she would at Acts in such a moment and said, "I am glad to meet you, Salmon." Klee looked momentarily over her shoulder inside the tent before turning to Joshua and Acts, saying quietly, "Will you have time to stay and have breakfast?"

Joshua quickly replied, "That sounds great!"

Klee took the moment to stare into Joshua's eyes. When she realized what she was doing she became slightly embarrassed. She smiled at him and turned to begin the food.

Acts looked at Salmon and said, "You know… You are staring at my sister?"

Salmon suddenly recognized what Acts had said, "I'm sorry. I didn't know that is what I was doing."

Joshua and Acts laughed at Salmon and as Klee came back with the food, she asked, "What are you laughing at?"

"Oh! Just the fact that you are so special, and we appreciate you making breakfast for us."

Joshua turned to the boys and said, "When you get through eating, fill your skins with water and we have to get going."

Klee stated, "To have this time with you is wonderful. You go do what you need to do and hurry back here."

He gave her a hug and started off to find Elishama, but not before almost tripping over the little lamb that always followed Klee. This brought a laugh and a shade of embarrassment for Joshua.

~

By the time Joshua reached the tribal leader, information had made its way from person to person and true to the form of gossip, most of that information was wrong. Joshua greeted Elishama, who was his uncle, and asked him to walk with him so they could talk.

Elishama fell into step beside Joshua. "I have overheard some people talking, and I must say I am concerned."

Joshua sighed in frustration. "Maybe the instructions you were given were not the right ones, Uncle."

"I want you to know, Joshua, I love you, and I am glad for the position you have with Moses. I would never do anything to hurt you. But the talk I have heard that we are to turn back and wait for the Egyptians is very alarming!"

Joshua began to laugh, softly at first, then building until he was almost bent over. Elishama stopped and stared dumbfounded at his nephew, but soon he began to laugh with Joshua, and after a few moments, Joshua was finally able to answer his uncle.

"I had not stopped to think about how things would change as they were passed around. And since you are my uncle, I will do my best to give you the accurate information." Joshua chuckled and started walking again. "We are to turn back, not to wait on the Egyptians, but to go to the place the Lord will meet with Moses, but only after we have been obedient in doing what He has told us through Moses."

"So, in turning around, we are being obedient?" The face of his uncle showed confusion. Elishama continued, "In case you hadn't noticed, it is in the direction of the Egyptians. The last report from the rear guard was that no one followed. Even so, the Egyptians are bound to find out we have turned back toward them, and it could give them the idea we might be coming back. I don't know how they would take that."

"Moses told me that he couldn't share all he had received from the Lord, and he doesn't know all the Lord God is doing. However, he is adamant that we go back to Pi Hahiroth between Migdol and the Red Sea. He told me; there the Lord God would bring glory to His name. He has done so much in delivering us from the Egyptians; it is hard to imagine what else He desires to do for us." Joshua finished.

Elishama relaxed and took a deep breath, slowing his pace some. "I know what I have seen, and I stand in wonder of the God we serve." He stopped and looked up into the pillar of cloud, "I used to live my life each day doing as I was told and not having anything to look forward to in the future. I feel I am off balance emotionally. I am just one man out of the millions of people. There are so few of us who even have the slightest understanding of worship to this God, the God of Jacob. Most of the people have fallen into serving the gods of Egypt over the generations. What can I do for my God that would be of any significance?"

Joshua smiled. "In my heart, I know Moses is the man God has chosen to lead the children of Israel, and I will support him in any way he needs. That is what you need to set in your heart as well,

Uncle. Let's work together to keep our tribe behind Moses all the way and do exactly what the Lord God tells us through him. We'll just take it one step at a time, I guess."

Elishama was a man of practicality. He thought if something made practical sense, it was worth doing. But he managed to extricate himself from that mode for a moment, and he began his pace again. He could see the young man's wisdom and how his time with Moses had given him direction and maturity. Elishama thought about the difference in having *no* choice in obedience and the choice to obey. What a great amount of trust was required to follow a God who had kept silent for generations! The future looked uncertain to a people who had, until only recently, no future at all and very little knowledge of God, except what was passed down from the first generation. They now had a choice in life. For the children of Israel, He was a kind and loving God who took them from slavery to a free people with a future, found only in Him.

Elishama sighed. "Joshua, I will do as you have learned and take life one step at a time. But uncertainty makes me nervous. In slavery, we always knew what to expect. Our God is a surprise every day."

"Good! That means we will have a true relationship with our God. I believe there is no limit to the possibilities!" Joshua could hardly contain himself. But he also realized five other tribal leaders waited for him, and they were not his relatives. As they walked toward the tent of Gamaliel and waited for the return of the others, their discussion soon began circling around their families. Elishama raised an eyebrow at Joshua. "So…have you had the chance to go by and see Klee?"

~

Meanwhile, Acts and Salmon had made the request to Gamaliel to host the meeting, and he assured them all would be taken care of. They reached the tent of Abidan in a shorter amount of time than was expected. After introductions, Abidan turned to grab his staff. He was an older man, older than any of the other tribal leaders and he had withstood much of the cruelty of the Egyptians. He also understood the appointed position of Moses. Abidan was a leader, and he had a very positive influence on his tribe. The fact that he followed Moses, because Moses followed God, was evident in his life and his speech.

After getting his staff, he struck out with a pace that Acts and Salmon had trouble matching. Abidan could hear their labored breathing, so he slowed his pace just enough so they could catch their breath and not lose much time in traveling to the meeting. Acts looked at Salmon and smirked. "Nice morning for a *brisk* walk."

"Brisk walk?" Salmon exclaimed. "This is almost a *run!*"

Abidan looked over at them, shook his head a little, grinned, and they all laughed.

Upon reaching Gamaliel's tent, the men all greeted each other, and Gamaliel motioned for them to eat the food his wife and daughters had prepared. As they began to eat, Elishama set the tone. "If you were offered the chance to return to the way we lived in Egypt or to obey what the Lord God has given us through Moses, what would be your choice?"

Gamaliel and Abidan exchanged glances before Abidan demanded, "Do I hear a challenge or a question that a child could answer? Of course, I would obey the Lord!"

"What life was there for us before the Lord God spoke?" Gamaliel added. "And now look at the life we have after He spoke and acted. He *is* the God of our future."

With that said, Joshua began. He laid out the parchment with the plans and instructions he had given to the other tribes, and before the meeting ended, good fellowship filled the tent.

Joshua arose from his seat. "If there are no questions, Acts, Salmon, and I will be on our way."

Abidan spoke up. "We will be ready for the sound of the ram's horn, Joshua. You just be ready for the pace we'll set." He cut a grin to Acts and Salmon.

Both of the boys laughed. Joshua looked confused, but he was content to let them laugh. With a smile, he put both of his hands out for Acts and Salmon and pulled them to their feet.

"Ready to go, my captain," Acts stated, followed quickly by Salmon, and off they went.

~

It was several miles to the tribe of Dan. After starting with a good pace, they slowed to a comfortable walk and not much was said for a while, but Acts finally broke the silence.

"Do you," speaking to both of them, "think Janue is cute?"

Joshua looked at Acts, the trace of a smile at the corner of his mouth. "I believe the question should be if Janue thinks *you're* cute."

Acts swallowed noisily. "That would be an appropriate question." He thought for a moment and then his eyes grew wide. "What if she doesn't think I'm cute? That could be bad."

They laughed. There was silence for a short moment. Salmon kicked a rock out of his path. "Yes, I think she's really cute, but I'm not interested in girls right now. I'm learning too much and really don't have time."

Joshua laughed as Acts suddenly realized what he had just vocalized.

Acts playfully punched Joshua in the arm. "You have no room to talk, Mr. I-can't-take-my-eyes-off-Klee."

Joshua grew quiet and rather red with embarrassment, but the younger boys took great delight in seeing their leader's response to their teasing. A mile of rest and the pace was picked back up.

~

The three reached the edge of the tribe of Dan as the sun shone down through the pillar of cloud. It had taken them longer to make the distance, because they had taken the time to move to the outside of the tribes to move past the people with ease. Joshua was not concerned about the time at this moment. He knew they would make it up on the way back to the front. He motioned with hand gestures for the three of them to bed down for the night. It had been a long couple of days, and they were all tired.

Joshua began sinking into sleep with thoughts of the deep blue eyes of Klee. He ran through his mind the many qualities she possessed and what a good wife and mother she would become. Maybe the boys were onto something. Those thoughts took him into dreams.

Salmon, on the other hand, kept thinking through the possibilities that came about from serving with Joshua and Acts. The things he wanted to learn and the opportunity to serve Moses himself was something he had never considered. Of course, he knew it had not been settled by Joshua that he would continue with them, but he had the desire and the heart to serve.

The friendship with Acts was something he had never encountered, either. To be so comfortable with a friend in such a short time was incredible. It was like acquainting himself to a brother he had always known. He knew in his heart there were many things' Acts could teach him, and at the same time, he also recognized several things he could help Acts understand. The foremost being Salmon would always love him as a brother and not turn his back on him. He knew Acts' heart ached for a father, one who loved him and encouraged him, and Salmon wanted him to see that in his own family. Salmon knew his father would take Acts in, just as if had been born to him. He understood Joshua was more of a "big brother" figure, and the hole in Acts' heart was left by Acts' own father. But it could be repaired with time and love. Salmon also knew his father would spend time listening as well as instructing, and with that confidence, Salmon knew Acts would be accepted into his own family.

Acts rolled over on his side, thinking of all the wonderful things he had seen the Lord God do. The ten plagues of Egypt, the Passover, and a miracle he had not considered much, due to the business of the days. The pillar of cloud by day and the pillar of fire by night. The cloud rose up so high in front of the company of Israel that its shadow was cast upon all the tribes. The air still burned hot during the day, but he knew that out from under the cloud, the sun could be disastrous for the very young and old, man or animal.

He thought of the first days of freedom and how the lamb they had eaten the night of Passover had been enough nourishment for the entire company to travel from Rameses to Succoth and then to Etham without stopping, day or night. While they had been camped at Etham, the pillar of fire was not as bright, yet still visible as a reminder to their company the Lord God traveled with them. Acts had heard no one grumble or speak of the distance traveled, partly out of fear the Egyptians would come after them, and partly because their minds were not aware of the distance with the thought of their newfound freedom.

The pillar of cloud could be seen for miles from the front to the rear of the company. At times, Acts would swear he saw it take shape and move like a man with a large sword in his right hand with the train of his cloak stretching to cover them. Acts liked to use his imagination to put shapes to clouds on a regular basis, but this was different. The pillar of cloud was the same shape every day. Even in his young experience, he knew it was a miracle. It not only seemed to guide them, but it moved ahead of them to lend its protection.

The pillar of fire was the more spectacular sight. Rising up like a tornado, the fire swirled around and, as it grew wider and higher, it stretched from the front of the company to the rear guard lighting the way for each person's step. It gave off enough heat to keep the Hebrews from freezing at night. Every once in a while, Acts looked up to the pillar of fire to see if he could recognize the figure of the man he saw in the pillar of cloud. He would squint at first and then open his eyes wide. He would see something similar to a sword turning in the hands of a warrior, only the sword moved at a speed which made it almost unrecognizable. Since reaching Etham, neither the cloud nor the fire had moved them forward. Acts knew that soon they would be moving again - moving toward a new future. He remembered how the sons of Israel had kept their promise to bring the bones of Joseph to be buried with his fathers in the land God had promised. The honor of carrying the bones of Joseph had fallen to the tribe of Judah. The Pharaoh during that time gave Joseph the Egyptian name of Zaphenath-Paneah, meaning savior. To carry the body which saved Egypt and the world from terrible drought and famine was an honor to last a lifetime.

Acts endeavored to remain awake in order to ponder more on such wonderful subjects, but sleep came to him, and such sweet sleep it was, not only for him, but for all three of them. As light edged the horizon, all of them awoke, stretched, and smiled at each other. They approached the soldiers standing at the edge of the camp with right hands held high, and the guards raised their hands in return, welcoming the travelers to the tribe of Dan.

Joshua spoke first. "How are the men of Dan this fine day in the deliverance of the Lord?"

The shorter and rather rotund guard puffed a bit. "To walk in the deliverance of the Lord is His blessing! Although I do miss baking my pies!" He looked very pleased and proud to proclaim that truth. "What brings you men our way?"

"I have news and instructions from Moses," Joshua replied.

"Then you must be Joshua, the servant of Moses!" exclaimed the short one.

The taller guard bowed slightly. "It is an honor to have you in our camp. Are you looking for Ahiezer, our tribal leader?"

"Yes," Joshua answered.

"Then we will take you to him," said the taller man.

"And find you something to eat," said the short one, whose round frame suggested that eating was never far from his mind. "I'm sure you are hungry."

His taller companion gave him a brotherly jab with an elbow. "That is because *you* are the one who is always hungry."

The short one blustered very noticeably and patted his round belly. "I just happen to have a very healthy appetite." He ignored the eye from his friend and gestured toward Joshua, Acts, and Salmon. "But I'm sure our guests are hungry, too, aren't you?"

The three nodded energetically.

They turned and followed the two men until they came to the tent of Ahiezer. He was an impressive man of height and muscle.

"Joshua!" Ahiezer boomed deeply as he reached out his right arm toward Joshua. The young man stepped forward and grabbed the man's forearm with his hand. Ahiezer smiled broadly. "What a pleasure to see you, my friend! How is your father? Doing well, I hope?"

"Oh, yes, Ahiezer, my family is well."

"And how about that uncle of yours?"

"Elishama is just as well," Joshua answered. The two men stared at each other for a brief moment, and to Salmon and Acts, it was like the grip of Ahiezer was to test Joshua's resolve.

Ahiezer let go of Joshua's arm and smiled. "Your strength is increasing." He gestured to the cushions in the center of the tent. "Come in. Sit down. We were just about to eat some bread and vegetables and have some goat's milk. Would you care for some?"

"Yes, sir, we would," Joshua replied, casting a glance at his two companions.

Ahiezer turned his broad gaze toward Acts and Salmon. "Who are these fine-looking, young men with you?"

Joshua turned and put his right hand on Acts' shoulder. "This is Acts of the same tribe as me," Joshua put his left hand on Salmon's shoulder, "and this is Salmon of the tribe of Judah, the son of Nahshon."

"Nahshon!" bellowed Ahiezer loudly. "Why that… he… well, he stole the girl I wanted for my wife!"

The visitors stood there, staring, soundless. Salmon's face immediately turned bright red. After a moment, Ahiezer winked at Joshua and said, "Of course, there are no hard feelings. How else would I have met the woman I have now?" His eyebrows bobbing up and down for emphasis.

The sound of the air in Salmon's lungs rushed out in a way everyone could hear. He turned even redder than before. Laughter filled the tent. Ahiezer motioned again for the cushions. "Sit down, boys, and tell me why you're here."

Joshua asked if he could send a couple of men to the tribes of Gad and Naphtali to request the presence of their tribal leaders for this meeting. He stressed the importance of the conference and the fact that the three of them had little time left to start their journey back to report to Moses. Ahiezer understood the gravity of the situation, and being a man of action, sent two men to fetch the tribal leaders. Joshua thanked him and sat down. Acts plopped down with Joshua and looked at him and asked, "We are not to go?"

Joshua smiled and said, "I knew these men would come at the invitation without hesitation. We need the rest for our run back to the front." It was then Joshua noticed Salmon still standing, staring at nothing, his face pink. Acts grabbed his hand and yanked him to the floor of the tent, bringing on another round of laughter.

A little boy and girl brought the bread and goat's milk to the men, and they began to eat. All three of the boys were very hungry, and although they did not converse much, Ahiezer was full of laughter and stories from the past few days. He was truly a breath of fresh air.

It was still very early in the morning, and Acts kept looking toward the front of the company. Salmon noticed his friend's behavior, and after looking back and forth from Acts to the direction Acts was staring, he finally asked loudly, "What are you looking at?"

Acts blinked at Salmon before returning his gaze again to the far front. "I want to watch the pillar of cloud begin to grow into the Angel of the Lord." That is what he had decided to call the change as he thought to himself, *'He is a God who will never leave me.'*

Pagiel, the tribal leader of Asher, and Ahira, the leader of the tribe of Naphtali, arrived long before the noon day meal was to be served. Joshua was astonished at the surprisingly short length of time that had passed, but Ahira explained, "I was at the tent of Pagiel when your messengers arrived. We came as soon as we heard of the meeting."

Pagiel nodded. "We are excited to hear what we are to do next. The tribes are full of freedom and ready to follow Moses wherever the Lord God leads."

Joshua looked back at them and wondered in his heart, '*Will they be as excited when they hear the orders?*' He sat up straight, took a drink of goat's milk, turned, and looked to each face. "The entire company of Israel is to turn back to camp near Pi Hahiroth, between Migdol and the sea. We are not to go through the land of the Philistine's. God has revealed to Moses that He intends to bring glory to His name through our obedience."

There was a long pause, and the leaders exchanged glances before turning their attention back to Joshua. Acts and Salmon felt uncomfortable, and their eyes flicked back and forth between Joshua and the others.

Ahiezer broke the silence. "Then we'd better get ready to go! I do have one question, though. How are we to accomplish such a task?"

Joshua explained everything while showing them the parchment, from the flag men to the different sounds of the ram's horn. Ahira nodded, "If those are the orders passed from the Lord God to Moses and to you, then those are the orders to be followed. Our God requires obedience, and we are men of discipline."

Pagiel agreed. "Where would our trust be if we did not obey? I'm so glad the Lord leads Moses. If all the tribal leaders were to come together and try to make plans, it would be... ridiculous."

Joshua let out a long, slow sigh, copied by Acts and Salmon. Joshua said, "The Lord has prepared the way for us, and He has once again amazed me through your willingness. The day is passing, and my two fellow soldiers and I must try and make it back to the front as soon as possible. If there are no questions, may we fill our skins with water and be on our way?"

There were no questions—only faces filled with gratitude. The three filled their skins, waved goodbye, and began what would be a long, slow run. It was somewhere around 23 miles back to Moses. Acts glanced up to the pillar of cloud to see his "Angel of the Lord" and smiled in his heart. Acts glanced at Salmon, then looked at Joshua, and in a low whisper asked, "Is Salmon to go all of the way with us, my captain?"

Joshua looked over at Salmon, who was in deep thought while running, and looked to Acts and said, "The Lord has shown He is worthy to serve with us, has He not?"

"Yes! He has, my captain."

"Then serve with us he will," Joshua finished.

As Acts ran, he could definitely feel, in his heart, the Lord was building a family around him.

CHAPTER 5

ACTS PUSHED

THE THREE COMPANIONS KEPT A steady pace as they passed back through the sea of people. The pillar of cloud provided shade, and there was even a light breeze blowing to their backs, pushing them forward to complete their task. They had fixed their course just to the edge of each tribe, which left virtually nothing in their way. The pounding of their feet and the rhythm of being in step seemed soothing, and the miles elapsed quickly. They would stop and drink while walking at a moderate pace, so they would not grow weak. They remained quiet most of the trip back. The focus level of each member of the trio was very high, and the silence was comfortable. They watched the sun move across the sky through the pillar of cloud.

The sun set, and as they continued toward the front, they each saw the pillar of fire appear, growing from a flame on the ground into a whirling tornado of fire that soared up and over, stretching from the front to the rear guard. It was a light by which to run and for the people to start getting ready.

Acts broke the silence of the run. "I know this may sound like a childish thing, but do either of you see the warrior in the pillar of fire with the spinning sword?"

The childlike trust Acts had in Joshua always brought the big brother out in him. "You know, I've only had the chance to really study the pillar for the first time in these past few days because of all the many tasks to be accomplished. Now, really taking time to look at its magnificence, I can see something in it that looks like a warrior with a sword." He paused and added, "And it looks like it is in His right hand with a handle so long it could be used with both hands." He was specific because he wanted Acts to know he wasn't making it up to just agree with him.

"I've seen it, too," Salmon chimed, "and I think the part of the pillar that stretches to the rear guard looks like a long flowing cloak or robe."

"That makes me feel better," Acts replied, "because, sometimes I think my mind goes way off and I feel there is no one else around. I am glad, I have someone to share these thoughts with."

"Well, little brother, you can always share with me," Joshua assured him. "You might get some laughter, but I will always listen and be honest." He paused for a moment and suggested, "Let's stop here for a while and take a short rest." They ran over to a water cart and asked if they could fill their skins and then went back to the edge of the tribe to sit down before getting back to the run. Joshua decided to not stop by and see his family on the way back so, by the end of that day, late in the evening, they had reached the edge of the tribe of Issachar, the second tribe. They slowed their pace to catch their breath so they could begin the report to Moses.

The tent of Moses stood on a hill at the very front of the children of Israel, positioned so he could look out over the plains at the tribes. With his staff in one hand, he raised the other as he saw Joshua and his two companions approaching. Moses was a tall and very handsome man hiding the number of years he had lived. He was the kind of person that commanded attention even if he did not ask for it. A big smile grew on his face, and then he laughed as he said, "The Lord God told me you would be here tonight." He opened his arms and wrapped them around Joshua.

"Oh, He did, did He?" Joshua answered as he returned Moses' embrace. Joshua took a step back and allowed Acts to step forward. His greeting was just as boisterous, "Acts, the Acts of good will! You look as if you have grown these past days. It's good to see you, my son!"

Acts put his arms around Moses and said, "I have grown, Moses. Not really in height, but in heart."

As Acts stepped back, Moses tilted his head and asked, "What part of his p-personality has he revealed to you?"

Acts took a moment to think before answering, "He truly loves these people. I have seen it in the care He provides in the pillar of cloud and fire. How He thinks of every detail and then hides it from me until it suddenly overtakes me."

"I would say you have grown indeed," Moses agreed. He turned his attention to the young man now standing beside Joshua. "And who is this fine young man?"

Joshua looked at Salmon, then back at Moses. "His name is Salmon, son of Nahshon and he is a soldier of the Lord. He is a faithful new friend who has come to serve with us, if you see that this is right."

Moses took a moment to look into the boy's eyes with a gaze that seemed to look into the very character of a man. "You have much s-strength," he said to Salmon after a moment of study, "and I can see you have much endurance—essential qualities for assisting with the task which rests on Joshua's shoulders. You are wise in choosing whom you follow." He paused for a moment and said, "You also have strong c-convictions in our God. I can see it in your eyes and in the way you stand palms open, arms to your side as if ready to listen and learn. If it is with us you wish to serve in taking care of the children of Israel, then serve with us you shall! Welcome, Salmon son of Nahshon." Moses reached out and gave Salmon a hug that felt just like a hug from his father.

Salmon stepped back and looked into the eyes of Moses and saw a humility that drew out of him the *desire* to serve. "Thank you, Moses. I will serve with obedience."

Salmon turned to Joshua and Acts. "Thank you, my friends. You have made me feel welcome from the first moment we met. It will be an honor to serve with you."

This brought a moment of celebration, and Moses said, "Come. Sit and we will eat. I know it is late and you will need to rest."

They all found a place on the soft skins in the tent and began to eat and drink. As they did, Moses asked Joshua, "How did the tribes take the instructions?"

Joshua sighed and took a sip of his grape juice before answering. "I am surprised to see such different personalities between the tribes. The attitudes set by the leaders of each tribe run through the veins of the entire group."

Moses never took his eyes off Joshua as he listened to him.

"The middle tribes surrounding the Levites had the most trouble accepting the instructions."

"Is it with the leadership of the Levites?" Moses asked.

"Yes," answered Joshua. "When Aaron is with you, Korah, Dathan, and Abiram want to be the tribal leaders, but they are quick to explain that their leadership comes into play only when Aaron is absent. They gave Acts and Salmon some trouble, but Acts took care of it." He smiled proudly at Acts. "The three men came to the meeting and listened, and Korah began to offer what he thought would be the 'easy way' to turn the tribes, but I did not allow him to continue. They heard the instructions and had no questions."

Moses thought for a moment, looked over at Acts, raised one eyebrow, and said, "In handling the situation with those men, I would say you've grown more than you said you had, Acts."

Acts grinned.

Moses turned back to Joshua. "My cousin, Korah, is hungry to be a leader." Moses seemed to sadden slightly. "He is my cousin, but not my friend." He looked over at Salmon and asked, "Were you with Acts when he encountered these men?"

"Yes, sir," Salmon answered.

Moses turned his gaze to Acts. "It is good the Lord had Salmon watching your back."

Acts smiled. "He not only watched my back, but he took care to watch the back of Eliasaph as well."

Moses looked back at Salmon and smiled. He did not remove his eyes from Salmon when he spoke to Joshua. "What do you think needs to be done concerning the leadership of the Levites, Joshua?"

Joshua knew that the Lord had already told Moses the answer and that this question was intended for Joshua's instruction. He cleared his throat. "None of these men have the experience, or the wisdom, to lead an entire tribe. God has chosen Aaron to be the tribal leader of the Levites. His heart beats for the Lord, and his wisdom is founded securely in his faith. Surely, he is the one to lead them, now that we are out of Egypt and on our way to the land God promised His people."

Moses sighed, turning his attention back to Joshua. "It is hard to see your own children take roads you never wanted them to take, but there comes a time when a parent must allow their children to stand alone and be held accountable for themselves. My brother is a humble man. I did not get to be around Nadab and Abihu as children. There are things fathers do out of frustration in a situation they would never do otherwise. It's easy to look b-back and say, 'I should have done this or that, but I know my brother was taught in a good way. He passed down the teachings to all of his sons; teachings that molded their personalities up to the p-point where each one can now stand individually as a man."

Moses looked off into the distance. "I have met Nadab and Abihu since my return, and I have also met two other very fine young men, Eleazar and Ithamar, who love the Lord God with all their heart. The experience of raising Nadab and Abihu gave Aaron much wisdom in raising Eleazar and Ithamar to their benefit. Nadab and Abihu are seeking to be like Korah and these other men. They are not lost; they just need guidance, which is why the Lord God has instructed Aaron personally to go back to his tribe and be the leader the Lord has called him to be. In time, the Lord will show all his sons what their role will be in the company of the children of Israel. We must trust and depend on *The Lord* to do the teaching *we* cannot."

Joshua slowly nodded. "I was starting to put blame on Aaron for the actions of his sons, but I see now they are grown men making their own decisions."

"Yes," Moses said. "It's something to think about. We better get some rest, because tomorrow is the start of a new journey, and it will be one in which the Lord God will glorify His name."

Joshua, Acts, and Salmon stood to go, but before they could leave, Moses rose to give them a hug and tell each one individually, "I love you."

~

They all slept well on the skins Moses provided just outside his tent. In the early morning, all awoke to the sound of Moses getting up and putting the finishing touch on his one bag of belongings. He required so little it was put on the back of a young camel he had been given by Joshua's father. Moses called for a young boy to take and lead the young camel as they walked through the day. The boy led the camel back to his father, who was a member of the tribe of Judah. Moses called Joshua and his young soldiers to breakfast, and while they were eating, he began to give each of them instructions for the day.

"I will walk in front of the tribe of Judah with the Angel of the Lord."

Acts slapped his legs and said excitedly, "I thought so! I *knew* I saw a warrior in the pillars!"

Moses laughed and asked, "You have seen Him in the cloud?"

"Yes! And in the fire, too!"

"We all see it," added Salmon.

Moses laughed before continuing. "You, Joshua, will stand on the large rock and meet each tribe so they will know you are to be the center of the turn. With the sound of your ram's horn, let them know when to begin the turn. Moses cautioned, "Make sure, as your own tribe begins to turn, that your family's needs are met."

Joshua looked at Moses and nodded to let Moses know he understood. If his mouth had not been full of bread, he would have answered Moses verbally. Moses turned to Acts and Salmon. "I want you to meet up with your own tribes before they get to the turn. I want you to check your families and then meet Joshua at the rock. As for you, Salmon, go to your father and ask him if I may have you assist Joshua in the responsibilities I pass to him. It would seem that you and Acts work well as a team."

"Yes, sir," Salmon answered.

Moses continued. "At the sound of the horn, the tribe of Judah will start moving to the east. Judah will start their turn now, since they are at the rock. Once they are around the rock, they will walk approximately another mile and then begin their second turn. This rock will serve as a hub for the entire tribe to keep their bearings. It will help keep the tribes together. He paused to allow the information to be understood, and he reached down to take a drink of water. He looked at each face and said, "Today will be a good day, and all will go as planned. Have faith in the Lord God, for it is He who has planned this day, even before Jacob and his family came to Egypt."

Joshua stood and helped Acts and Salmon to their feet. "I guess I will see both of you at this rock as our tribes come to the turn."

At that moment, Acts' hand flew to his ear. Joshua quickly wrapped his arms around Acts just before he started to fall back into a deep dream.

~

Dust, like dust from a storm coming from behind; deep darkness. Acts could see water, deep and blue ahead of him. Sounds of battle behind him, coming toward him, then a mighty wind, powerful, from the east. It was blowing so hard; he was having trouble standing. People running in panic; the snake of mist that was in Egypt—appeared. It was turning its eyes once more to Acts. He felt the fear well up in his heart as it did back in Egypt that dark night. The Snake Mist wanted to kill Acts but did not approach him. Acts felt a hand on his shoulder. He could see that the Snake

Mist now gave the man his attention. The man had a scar all of the way through his hands. As Acts started to look at this man, he could see the same kind of scars were in his feet. The man looked like a warrior and showed no fear with the Snake Mist. He pointed and at once the Snake Mist left. Acts' breathing increased and at that moment, he opened his eyes.

Joshua looked down into his eyes. "You're okay. It's over. Just be still for a moment."

Acts blinked until the images around him came into focus. "I didn't even feel it coming."

Moses bent down and put his hand on the forehead of Acts. "You saw images?"

"Yes," answered Acts.

"Do they frighten you?"

"Sometimes they do, and sometimes they don't."

"But this one did," Moses said.

"Yes."

"You are very sensitive to the Lord, Acts," Moses said, standing back up. "His desire is that all men would be as sensitive. Don't be afraid of the dreams, for the Lord Himself is guiding you. I don't know how long you will see them, but I do know you see things in a light that is partly from the past and partly from the future. When the time is right, you and I will sit and discuss these things you have seen. I will go to the Lord and stand there for you."

"Thank you, Moses. I will try and not be afraid. It's just that they seem so real."

"I know," Moses said tenderly. "Be strong and have c-courage. Your strength will not fail."

Moses and Joshua helped Acts to his feet. Acts turned to Joshua and said, "Ready to serve, my captain."

As they turned to go, Joshua pulled Acts close to speak in his ear. "When you see Klee, tell her I am thinking of her, will you?"

Acts smiled and replied just as quietly, "Of course, I will! She will be glad to hear anything from you, Joshua."

Acts turned and ran to catch up to Salmon. Salmon looked at Acts and said, "Something about Klee?"

Acts grinned. "Yes."

Salmon returned his smile and looked ahead. "Thought so."

Moses looked out over the plains and amazement filled his heart. *"Only You, O Lord, could bring about such a wondrous thing in so many lives."*

Moses turned to Joshua and could see the concern he had for Acts.

Joshua took a deep breath. "I feel for Acts."

Moses looked into Joshua's eyes and smiled comfortingly. "Be at ease, my friend. We serve a loving God who works with purpose in all of His ways. He won't let anything happen to Acts that is not in accordance with His will."

Joshua shifted his weight. "Acts and his sister have come to mean a lot to me."

"Yes, I know," said Moses, a twinkle appearing in his eyes, "and they will come to mean more, especially his sister."

Joshua smiled rather sheepishly. "It's hard to hide it."

"Hide it!" laughed Moses. "If you're trying to hide it, my son, you're not doing very well! You may as well be honest with yourself and stop wasting time."

Joshua turned red.

Moses chuckled. "Now don't get embarrassed. I remember what it's like to walk the way of love."

A fleeting moment passed as Moses missed his wife and sons. They had returned to his father-in-law, Jethro, while Moses made the dangerous trek out of Egypt. But Moses turned his attention back to the nation of Israel. "It's time to turn. Blow the ram's horn, Joshua. Blow the horn to continue our journey to the Promised Land."

Joshua put the horn to his lips and blew the signal with clarity and accuracy. A shout of excitement sounded from the tribe of Judah, and they echoed back the same tune as it passed through the tribe like ripples in a pond from a pebble. The task of turning the tribes had begun.

~

Camels and donkeys loaded with all kinds of plunder the Egyptians gave to expedite the Hebrews out of Egypt passed by Joshua.

Joshua had instructed the flagmen to maintain eye contact with the next man holding the flags for boundaries and messaging. The women and children were in their position to the inside part of the turn and runner's flags could be seen throughout the tribe. When the signal came back to Joshua that the tribe of Judah was one mile east of the rock, he would listen for the second signal from Judah to start north, and to keep walking, slowly. They couldn't run off and leave the other tribes. And there needed to be room for the approaching tribes. Knowing the tribe of Judah consisted of 74,600 men, twenty years old or more, plus the additional women and children, caused Joshua to consider the amount of time needed to make the turn between the tribes. As the tribe of Judah began to walk east, it was overwhelming to watch such a large number pass by him. They raised their hands and staff and yelled at the top of their voices. The width of the tribe was wider than Joshua could see. The tribal leader approached Joshua straight-on, so the rock on which Joshua stood stayed centered with the turn around him.

~

Acts and Salmon met with Salmon's father. It was a welcome greeting as father and son wrapped their arms around each other.

"I have missed you, Salmon. And by the sound of the horn, I take it all went well?"

"Yes, sir. I am glad to see you." Salmon hugged his father again. "Where is Mother?"

"I'm right here."

Salmon immediately ran over and embraced her.

Acts started to turn and leave, but Nahshon took him by the arm and pulled him close. Acts almost fell into the hug he needed so desperately at that moment. Nahshon squeezed him. "And where were you going, Acts? It is just as good to see you, too."

"Thank you," Acts said, blushing slightly. "It is good to see you both."

At that point, Salmon's mother walked over, and as she hugged Acts, she whispered in his ear, "I thank you for watching over my son. You are truly a good friend. I can tell these things, you know? I'm a mother."

Acts smiled. "He is a good friend to me."

Salmon walked over to Acts and said, "I will see you later. Give my greetings to Klee."

"I'll be sure that Klee gets the message," Acts replied as he turned with a mischievous grin. "If Janue and Shade are around I'll tell them, 'hello' for you. And as he walked away, Salmon yelled after him, "Don't get carried away or anything."

Acts never turned around to look at Salmon, but raised a hand and yelled, "Oh, I won't."

Salmon turned to his parents, who were standing together with smiles on their faces. "I guess my whisper wasn't actually a whisper, was it?"

Nahshon raised an eyebrow. "Shade and Janue…. hmm?"

~

It took a while for the last of the tribe of Judah to make the mile marker to the east. Joshua could see the tribe of Issachar slowly advancing toward the rock on which Joshua stood. He could see Nethanel walking toward him. Joshua raised his hand, and Nethanel raised his in return.

"Is it time?"

Joshua smiled. "Yes, Nethanel, it is time. I was just about to sound the horn."

Nethanel's face turned serious. "I certainly hope we are doing the right thing. It doesn't feel right to me, turning back toward the place from which we are fleeing."

"What do we have to fear with the God of Abraham, Isaac, Jacob, and Joseph on our side?" Joshua asked. "He has shown His might and power, so if He tells us to turn back, He has the plan that is best for us, does He not?"

"Well, when you put it that way. The tribe is ready whenever you are, Joshua."

Joshua frowned slightly as he turned away. *"Kind of an odd way to be on such a wonderful journey"* he thought. *"Doubt is the one thing we* don't *need."* He raised the horn to his lips and gave the signal to Issachar.

Joshua thought for the next few hours about the doubt of Nethanel. It troubled him, and he prayed, "Lord, remove his doubt and show him how to put his faith in You." It took two and a half hours for Issachar to make the turn and reach the mile marker. When Joshua saw the marker had been reached, he turned to see the tribe of Zebulun approaching the rock and thought, "I hope they are more positive than Nethanel."

~

With the tribes walking toward him, Acts reached his home tribe just after the noon hour and was looking for Klee when, from around the corner of a water cart, his father came wobbling toward him. He looked very rough and sleep deprived. He saw Acts and yelled, "Get out of here! You are useless, and I don't want you around!"

"But why?" replied Acts. "What have I done to warrant such an action?"

"You embarrassed me in front of the men I stand with. You are a disgrace, and if you come around again, you will get the beating of your life. I threw some of your things in this bag. I'm not carrying it. Good riddance."

"Where is Klee?" demanded Acts.

"She is doing what I told her to do, and that's all you need to know. Now get out of here before I get my hands on you!"

Acts knew it would be very difficult to take his father in a fight. He was hefty, even more than three times Acts' weight. Though most of his father's bulk was not muscle, he could still do great damage before Acts could overtake him. Acts turned to go, picking up the bag and peeking inside. Not much occupied the bag: a cloak, another shirt, and a pillow Klee had made him. He walked away without looking back, now even more determined to find Klee. He began asking some of the people nearby for information about Klee's whereabouts, but not where his father could see him.

Acts approached an older man and woman on the other side of a few camels, which were loaded with their belongings. He respectfully inquired, "Excuse me, but could I ask you a question?"

"You already did, son," the old man replied, laughing at his own joke. Looking more carefully at the boy, he questioned, "Acts? Is that you?"

"Yes, sir." Acts answered.

"Where you been, boy? You've been the talk of this area for a while."

Acts frowned. "Talk? What talk?"

"About what you did to Korah. You stirred up an ant hill for sure and for certain. Your father yelled for hours, threw stuff, and pushed your sister around when she tried to get him to settle down."

Acts felt an anger he did not know existed from his usually calm spirit, and he did not let the man continue before blurting, "My sister? Where is she now?"

"Don't know, really. He sent her to somebody, but we never heard who."

"Was she, alright?" Acts was upset and worried. The expression of his face and tone of his voice clearly showcased his feelings.

The older man placed a hand on Acts' shoulder. "Now, settle down. She looked and sounded alright. Maybe she went to one of your brothers or sisters?"

Acts thought for a moment. "The only one I can think of she would have gone to would be my oldest brother. He's the only one who ever came to see us, even though that was several years ago. I don't even know where his wagon would be."

The old lady pointed toward the rear of the tribe. "I think she ran off crying over that way, yesterday."

"Thank you." Acts said, and he took off running. He ran a zigzag pattern down through the tribe, hoping to cover more area and have a better chance of spotting her. His emotions threatened to burst out of control, while tears stung his eyes and impaired his vision. He ran into a fat man about his height and was knocked backwards to the ground.

"Acts!?" the fat man hissed. It was his oldest brother, Gaph. Gaph was not blessed with the good looks that Klee and Acts shared, and he always smelled strongly. "Get up, boy! You're not hurt! After all, you took on Korah, didn't you?"

Acts got up into a stance, ready to fight. He had seen his brother from a distance several times and knew he was disgustingly fat and slow. At this point in his high emotion and the worry for Klee, he was even ready to go back to his father's tent and see about that beating.

"Where is Klee?" Acts demanded.

Gaph laughed with sarcasm. "You don't know? She was taken to Korah because our father knew you would come to find her. I guess we'll see just how much a man you are now, huh?"

Acts' patience could take no more mockery. He raised his right leg and kicked his foot under Gaph's chin with enough force to throw Gaph on his back. He leaned over Gaph and stared into his eyes. Acts voice was low and threatening. "If she is hurt, I will be back to see you, and then we'll see how 'little' of a man I am."

Gaph lay in a daze. Several other people stood around with the pretense of gathering their things, but mostly watching to see what would happen next. Acts jerked his head up and looked around, causing a sudden revival of activity from the witnesses, and they quickly went back to their business.

Acts needed to think. Joshua had taught him bad choices were made out of rage, but righteous anger could be used as a tool if the warrior allowed himself to be driven by *it* and *not* rage. He walked back through the tribe trying to maintain the previous pattern he used searching for Klee. He walked toward a water cart, his breathing hard and labored. As he walked, he tried to control his intake of air by inhaling slowly. When he reached the cart, his mind was a little clearer. He remembered to ask permission to have some water. The man leading the cart had a tender heart. "Is water all you need," he asked, "or do you need something else?"

Acts looked up and saw the face of a man scarred with the stripes of a whip. His eyes were kind, which helped Acts calm down a little. "My father doesn't want me, my brothers and sisters, except one, hate me, and I've lost the only sister who loves me."

"Sounds like you need a friend." The man handed him a cup of water. "I give you this cup of water in the Name of the Lord Most High."

Acts thought for a moment and said, "I have never heard that before. Who are you, if I may ask?"

The man smiled. "I am of the Tahanite clan, and my name is Kemuel. I serve the Lord Most High and His servant Moses."

Acts took a long, slow drink of water and thought his way back to what was happening. "Do you think the Lord God will lead me to my sister?"

"Well, let me ponder. Your father doesn't want you; your brothers and sisters hate you...who are you?"

"I am Acts, the servant of Joshua, the servant of Moses."

"Then *you* are the young man everyone is speaking of. And since you are that young man," he paused for a moment before continuing, "I believe you are a man of wisdom and valor, for anyone who would stand up to any of Korah's group is a leader. You must love Joshua and Moses?"

Acts felt grateful for this encounter. "Yes, I do. Can you help me find my sister?"

"Finding your sister won't be the problem. She will be seated between Korah and Abiram, and, most likely, the sons of Aaron. They will be ready for you, and I don't think they like you very much."

Off to the side, a man listened very intently to the conversation, and it caught Acts' attention. He turned to face the man straight on and recognized an Egyptian. He was about Acts' height, very muscular and handsome in appearance. Kemuel motioned for the man to come closer, and Acts could see that he was about the same age as Joshua.

Kemuel introduced him. "This is my adopted son, Telok. He was part of the imperial guard of Pharaoh, but he was friends with someone you know, and in that friendship, he came to understand why we serve the God we serve and became a Hebrew in heart. I took him, and he became my son. I believe the Lord God gave him to me, because I have no sons of my own, and my wife died in Egypt."

Acts offered his hand. "I am Acts, and I am very glad to meet you, Telok." Telok reached out and took Acts by the forearm. "It is said, "Tee-lok". And I am glad to meet the man Joshua picked as the one to stand with him."

Acts smiled and Kemuel exclaimed, "It is good to see a smile!"

Telok frowned slightly in concern. "I overheard you explaining your situation and would like to offer my assistance, if my father will agree." Telok looked to his father and the older man gave him a nod of permission.

Kemuel replied, "If that is what you feel, and you understand what is right and wrong in this situation, I leave you to the wisdom I have taught you. May the Lord Most High smile upon you and give you great success."

Acts breathed a long sigh and thought, *Down to the smallest detail. Thank you, my Lord God*. He said to both of the men, "My captain, Joshua, and another he has chosen to serve with us are waiting at the rock where he gives the signal. They will be in this camp soon. I think we should wait until they have joined us before taking action. I know that my captain has a *very* special interest in this matter."

"Good decision, Acts," agreed Kemuel. "I can see your training with Joshua has served you well. It is much the same as what Telok and Joshua had instilled into them."

Telok nodded. "I am looking forward to seeing the look on Joshua's face when he sees me. I was not able to find him before, and he does not know I follow with your people."

"It will be fun to watch that," Acts agreed. But in his heart, he battled with his thoughts. He could not understand why this was happening. *'Is the Lord with me? Is His love as real as I thought it was in these past days since leaving Egypt?'* He shook off the questions, because they did not even feel right passing through his mind. He knew what he had seen God do, and all He was doing. It was not only the stories he had heard growing up about the God of Abraham that created a hope in his heart. It was now a full-fledged faith birthed through the act of walking each day to learn more of God and the way He sees things. The questions still floated in Acts' thoughts and many different feelings wavered in his heart, but he was determined to stand in his faith and not be moved by mere emotions. He did not understand this situation, but he committed his heart to the Lord and thanked Him for his new friends.

CHAPTER 6

RESCUE

Joshua could see that Issachar was at the mile marker and they were turning back to the north now. As Joshua looked back at the tribe of Zebulun, he could see they were in line with his position, so he sounded the signal. It took Issachar more time to make the turn and get to the mile marker than Joshua had planned. Joshua waved to Eliab, but he did not come down to speak to him. Eliab understood he was trying to make the best of the time. Eliab even picked up his pace just a little and that did help. They walked for two hours when the tribe of Zebulun reached the mile marker, they followed Issachar to the north.

Joshua was beginning to think more and more of Klee and the question he would soon ask. The time between tribes gave him plenty of time to think that what Moses said was right. There was no need for any more time wasted. He loved Klee and wanted to take care of her and be the best husband he could be for her. All that remained was asking her father for her hand, and Joshua had no idea what he would require in payment. It was the way of his people. The only exception would be if her father was a danger to her. Joshua had considered it a distinct possibility because of the outbursts of anger, his friends, and habits he supported.

Joshua soon turned his thoughts back to those deep blue eyes and the smile that had captured his heart.

It was in the evening hours by the time Zebulun made it to the mile marker. Joshua knew with each passing tribe; Klee would be that much closer. Joshua could hardly wait until he could sound the signal for the tribe of Reuben to turn, and that would bring the tribe of Ephraim that much closer.

With Zebulun through the turn and out to the mile marker, the tribe of Reuben took the rest of the night to reach the mile marker.

He knew that Salmon would not leave his family until they were taken care of, and his father gave him permission to come back to him. He served with Joshua, but Salmon was still under the authority of his parents, and Joshua understood and respected this. He didn't know what was taking him so long to return, but he knew he would as soon as he could.

Joshua sounded the signal for the tribe of Simeon to begin their turn. He thought he would have time to make a quick run to see Klee before the tribe of Ephraim made it to the turning point. His running turned to walking, and as he entered his tribe, many people greeted him along his way. He found his clan and his father, and they spent a few moments in reunion. In doing as Moses asked, his time for visitation was very short. His mother and father knew of his duties. They had given him to the Lord long ago. After a drink with some bread and vegetables, Joshua was off to find Acts and Klee. He wanted to walk with them for as long as possible before he blew the signal again. He soon found the further back he ran, the heavier the mood became. Joshua began to notice people watching and pointing, and this brought him to a walk. He began to have the uneasy feeling that something was not right. He switched to hunter mode, keeping his senses keen as he moved through the people and animals, drawing less attention by slowing his pace. He even pulled his cloak up over his head so that his face was shadowed.

He was moving from one side of the tribe to the other when he saw Klee's father. He traveled with two donkeys carrying his tent and other belongings, but neither Klee nor Acts were with him. He walked slower and stayed behind some carts studying the situation. Her father walked in such a way that it appeared he had to hang on to the donkeys in order to even stand. The animals were simply following the others that were in front of them. Some men that associated with her father walked near, but no one involved themselves in any conversation. Joshua moved slowly around him looking for Acts, Klee, or somebody he knew. As he stepped around some cattle pulling a wagon, he saw Acts walking slowly beside the wheel of a water cart, but as he moved toward Acts, he felt a presence move behind him. Spinning around with his hands out for battle, he saw a dark-skinned face. He threw the cloak off of his head. "Telok? Is that you?"

Telok smiled and said, "You are still very much the hunter, aren't you, Joshua?"

At the sound of Joshua's voice, Acts started looking for him. Joshua could see by the look on his face something was very wrong. "Little brother, what is wrong?"

Acts was fine until Joshua called him "little brother." His throat constricted, and his eyes welled with tears. Joshua turned to Telok. "Telok, you tell me what's wrong. Where's Klee?"

Telok looked at Joshua's hot face and sweat-beaded forehead. "While I tell you, let me get you some water and then we will discuss the matter." Telok turned and dipped out some water and handed it to Joshua. Joshua knew Telok very well and trusted him completely. He took a long drink, giving Acts some time to pull his emotions together. Telok began, "The news of Acts and his encounter with Korah has spread throughout the clans in the tribes of Manasseh."

Joshua looked at Acts and then back to Telok as the Egyptian continued. "It would seem our young friend has made some enemies, including his own father."

Joshua looked back to Acts. "Did he hurt you?"

"No, my captain. Not physically."

Joshua could read the deep pain in Acts' eyes and held out his arms. Acts put his arms around Joshua and hugged him, drawing strength from the man he loved and admired.

Joshua held Acts out at arms' length. "Are you able to tell me what happened now?"

Acts nodded slowly. "As I approached my father, he started shouting at me to 'get out,' because I had embarrassed him in front of his friends, and he never wanted to see me again. He said if I came back around, I would 'get the beating of my life.' When I asked about Klee, he only grew angrier, so I left to go find my oldest brother, because I thought she might be with him. He told me she would be traveling with Korah because my father knew I would go there to find her. I guess Korah is waiting to return the favor."

Joshua cut his eyes to Telok's and asked, "And where do you stand in all of this, my friend?"

Telok looked at Joshua, "What is your command, my captain?"

Joshua thought for a moment of the irony of the switched roles because in Egypt, Telok was the captain. "They do not know when Acts is to return, nor do they know my interest in the matter. And you, my friend," he smiled at Telok, "they have no idea of you or your capabilities."

Acts spoke up. "There is another who shares interest in this matter."

Joshua snapped his fingers. "Salmon! Yes, of course."

"Who is Salmon?" asked Telok.

"He is another young warrior who loves Klee as though she were his own sister," Joshua explained. "Having the four of us puts the advantage in our favor, despite the fact they are not acting in a manner worthy of the Lord. They will only be looking for Acts. We don't have to act hastily unless they pose a threat to Klee physically. Acts, you will move slowly and speak with a calm voice. Wait to see what level of interest and loyalty the others who are there with Korah have in this matter. There is no need to go charging in. With your actions so deliberate, it may put Korah into a mode of thought that makes him overconfident, giving us the edge." He thought for a moment and counted off the number of men he knew would be there. "Korah, Abiram, Dathan, Nadab, and Abihu are sure to stand with him and probably a few more."

"'Overconfidence creates bad judgment,'" Telok recited.

"Right," said Joshua. "Salmon is due to meet me at the rock soon." He glanced toward Acts. "He was going to check in with his parents and then meet me. But he doesn't know where we are right now. I will go back to the front of the tribe to give the signal and wait for Salmon there as we planned. The movement of the turn will only help us to blend in with the rest of the tribe. The Levites are traveling dispersed throughout the tribe of Manasseh, so they shouldn't notice the four of us lagging behind at different points and mixing in with their tribe. Pull your cloaks over your heads and move slowly on the outside edge of the tribe. Start moving toward Korah and his group when you see them. Acts, make your way to the middle so you can approach them directly. All of their attention will be on you."

Despite his efforts to hide it, Joshua's eyes showed anger that this matter even existed. He looked at Telok. "I can't tell you how good it is to see you, my friend, especially under these circumstances. Acts and Salmon are quite capable, but they lack experience. They will learn much today."

Acts turned to Joshua. "I have already learned much." Looking at Telok he said, "It is strange how such a situation can make me feel we have known each other all our lives. My heart trusts you completely, and I cannot help but feel a bond with you, an Egyptian, in the Lord Most High." Acts spoke not in a demeaning manner, but amazement that the Lord could use anyone for His purposes.

Telok took no offense, but rather corrected Acts politely, "A new Hebrew, if you will."

"Oh, yes!" said Acts. "I'm sorry; a bond with a new Hebrew."

Telok smiled. "I feel more comfortable with that."

"I will return to the front to give the signal for the tribe of Gad to turn and watch for Salmon," Joshua announced. "If he does not come back before Elishama, the tribal leader passes me, I will return, and we will proceed as planned with the three of us. Agreed?"

Telok and Acts both nodded in agreement.

Joshua continued, "This is the last clan to make the turn in the tribe of Gad. I will sound the signal for Ephriam to begin the turn when they reach the mile marker. Manasseh will be a while getting to the rock. I will sound the signal for them to begin the turn and then return to you. I know that Moses told me not to turn my back on these men. Even in the midst of such a wonderful time, there will always be those who do not see the wonders of the Lord God; they will only see what they can gain."

"We will wait for you," Acts assured him.

Telok smiled in concurrence with Acts as Joshua turned, pulled his cloak over his head, and started moving at a moderate pace back to the front. He moved to a position between two clans where he would be less noticeable and able to move without obstacle.

Telok smiled at Acts. "Now comes the hard part."

"What's that?" asked Acts.

"The waiting."

Joshua made it to the rock with time to spare as the tribe of Gad reached the mile marker, he would sound the signal for Ephriam. He was now waiting for the tribe of Manasseh to approach the rock to begin their turn. Here is where he would meet Acts and Telok. When Joshua saw Gamaliel he asked, "Is the leader of the tribe of Manasseh ready to begin the turn?" And with a sign of conformation Joshua placed the ram's horn to his lips but did not find the pleasure he had before. His mind was busy planning and preparing for what might lie ahead. At that very moment, he heard a familiar voice. "Joshua!" Salmon shouted in greeting.

The smile that came across Salmon's face faded when he saw Joshua's eyes. "What is wrong, my captain?"

Joshua filled Salmon in on the situation. "This is something that can quickly go from moderately good to very bad. We will have to be very alert, and even though you haven't had much time to train with us, I have the utmost confidence in you."

"The Lord has trained my hands to defend; and defend I will. Klee is like my sister."

Joshua looked back with a half-smile. "I knew you would say that."

Together, they turned to walk back into the tribe of Manasseh. By pulling their cloaks over their heads, they moved with a slow, even pace to meet up with Acts and Telok. In the mass of faces, they blended in easily.

Time seemed to pass slowly for Acts and Telok as they moved with the front of the tribe. Telok's eyes finally caught sight of Joshua and said to Acts, "Is this Salmon with Joshua?"

"Yes," said Acts.

"He looks every bit the warrior you described," Telok confirmed.

As Joshua and Salmon approached, Telok and Acts fell into step beside them, pulling their cloaks over their heads. As they approached the second half of Manasseh, Joshua said, "Salmon and I will make our way to the right edge of the center. Acts, you will move up the middle, because I would expect Korah and Abiram to be nowhere else except the center. Telok, you take the left side of center. Stay within eyesight of the situation. Keep your eyes on Korah, Abiram, and Dathan or any others that seem to be close by. Look at their walk, the way they hold their hands and if they do or do not have weapons. If you focus on Klee, you will lose sight of what you need to see." Joshua looked at Acts to make sure the younger man understood. "Remember: the righteous anger—not the rage—will prevail."

All nodded and began moving to the assigned positions. Joshua began thinking to himself, "*Keep your eyes on Korah and not on Klee. Maintain focus.*" He knew it would be hard, not only for him, but for Acts and Salmon as well. He did not worry about Telok, because he knew Telok was an experienced warrior.

Joshua and Salmon moved in and out of the edge of the tribe, keeping Acts in sight, as did Telok. As they began their approach to the back of the tribe, they saw Acts start his approach toward Korah. Acts saw Klee following Abiram with a rope around her hands to lead her. Her hair was a mess and her face dirty, but he could see no bleeding. *'They better thank the Lord God she has not been hurt,'* Acts thought darkly.

The group of men with Korah hung back toward the very end of the tribe, so that other people in the tribe would not interfere. The farther back they walked, the less attention they drew to Klee in the first place. It was a few more moments before Abiram looked up and saw Acts approaching.

"Well, the young soldier returns to claim his sister," Abiram sneered.

Four men on Telok's side began to spread out, and Telok thought to himself, *'Only four, and I thought this would be a challenge.'*

Five more men on Korah's other side began to move out to surround Acts, not noticing Joshua and Salmon behind them.

Abiram pulled Klee up harshly, trying to stir up anger in Acts. But Acts kept approaching them in a slow, deliberate manner, just as Joshua had instructed.

Korah seemed to be confused at the calm approach of this young man. "You might feel somewhat confident in regard to our last meeting, but I can assure you, I will not be taken by surprise again. You are going to be taught a lesson. I know I cannot kill you, but I can certainly make you wish I had."

Klee began to speak, but Acts looked at her and shook his head slightly. As she studied his face, she realized there was more to the situation than what appeared. She never took her eyes off Acts, so that no one else would be tempted to look around the arena in which she had been placed.

"Why do you have my sister bound up like she is a prisoner?" Acts spoke in a calm, soft voice.

"Prisoner?" mocked Korah. "She's no prisoner—only bait to catch an irritating little dog that nipped my heel." Laughing, he turned to look at all his "pack" to gain confidence, because he knew deep inside, he could not take this young warrior of Joshua's alone.

"If you want your sister," he said, yanking her close, "come and get her."

Acts paused for a moment. "I wonder what Joshua would say about this if he knew how you were treating someone *very* special to him in such a harsh manner?"

Fear flashed in the eyes of those around Klee. Korah quickly pointed out, "Joshua's at the front of the tribes giving the signal for the turn. He knows nothing of our little problem. My men have been watching for him or any other you might have enlisted, and they have found that you are alone."

"Well then, Korah, why don't you and I settle this? I'll walk forward to get my sister, and you can just let her go and this will end in peace." Acts was able to speak exactly as Joshua had told him. But this seemed to only enrage Korah.

"You think you can talk to me like I am some child? *No!* We will have this out, and you will taste the beating that belongs to you *and* your sister!" Korah threw Klee to the ground, and she landed hard on her side, knocking the wind from her.

It took all that Joshua had in him to stay in position and not kill Korah where he stood. But he knew he had to let Acts have the next move.

Klee hit the ground from the pull of the rope, and Acts instinctively moved toward her. As he did, Korah ran at Acts in a fit of rage, shoving his shoulder into Acts' chest, lifting him off the ground, moving him backward several feet. Acts landed hard on his back.

Acts had taken his attention off Korah for only a second, and as he fought to draw breath into his lungs again, he thought, '*That won't happen again.*'

As Korah ran toward him a second time, Korah picked up his right foot as he would to squash a bug, intending to put it in the middle of Acts' face. Acts rolled to his right, just in time to let Korah push his foot into the dirt. Acts then rolled back onto Korah's foot and brought up his elbow into the back side of Korah's knee, pitching the bigger man to the ground.

Acts rolled away from Korah and got to his feet.

Joshua grabbed Salmon's arm to keep him from giving away their position and joining the fight.

Salmon understood what Joshua was doing for him, and he pulled himself back, though it was hard for him not to jump in the middle of it.

Acts was now between Abiram and Korah, with Klee behind Abiram. Abiram approached Acts on his right side.

'*Bad idea*', Joshua thought.

Acts brought his foot up and pushed it into Abiram's chin, lifting him up and off of his feet. Acts turned to meet Korah straight on. The other men who stood with Korah did not approach the action at this point, knowing Korah would take it as an insult to his pride if they interfered with his revenge.

Acts rolled forward on his shoulders toward Korah, and as his feet started to come over his body, the scene seemed to almost stop in the mind of Acts. He completed his roll and time resumed. Acts planted his left heel into the middle of Korah's chest, knocking him to the ground beside Klee. Acts stood over Korah.

It was at this point Dathan, one of the four men closest to Telok, decided to get involved. He pulled his arm back to hit Acts in the side of his head, but the man's arm could not come forward. As he turned to see what held him, his eyes opened wide in silent fear as he met the eyes of an Egyptian. Telok pulled Dathan toward him and shoved his elbow into the man's jaw, flipping him out of the way without drawing the attention of the other three.

On the other side of Acts, two of the men started to approach Acts from behind. Joshua bumped Salmon's arm and they both sprang into action.

Acts took a quick glance at Salmon and the scene froze again. Acts could see the dust in the air nearly halt and the movement of Salmon in slow motion, then time resumed. Acts saw Salmon finish tackling one man from behind. As Salmon crashed into his target, the two men on his right noticed the new threat and moved toward the boy.

Joshua, still unnoticed by the two reacting to Salmon, grabbed the man closest to him, catching him by the hair on the back of his head and pulling him back with such force the man's feet left the ground. Joshua released his hold, and the man's momentum carried him further to land flat and hard on his upper back, forcing all the wind from his lungs. Joshua turned, threw the hood off his head, and moved to help Salmon up from the ground.

Korah had reestablished his footing, intending to make a play toward Acts again. He pulled his arm back to strike Acts. As the man's arm became fully extended, Acts grabbed Korah's wrist with his hand and placed his opposite hand on the man's elbow, pulling Korah toward his side. Using his momentum, Acts' lifted Korah up and threw him, allowing Korah to land on his chest once again in front of Klee. Korah's eyes met hers and she gave a hint of a smile. This infuriated Korah.

With Acts' attention now on Klee, and with Korah on the ground in front of him, Abiram moved in close enough to ram his fist in the back of Acts' head and knocked the boy to the ground beside Korah.

Salmon jumped to his feet as Joshua appeared at his side. The two remaining men rushed both of them. Salmon pulled back just enough to see Joshua's intentions. Joshua crossed in front of Salmon to the closest man, blocked a punch, threw the man's arm down, and struck him in the throat. Salmon watched and mimicked his captain in dealing with the other man, leaving both men on the ground struggling to breathe.

Telok grabbed the two men closest to him by the back of their hair. One was Nadab and the other Abihu. With one in each hand, he pulled them backwards, as if they were made of wheat. He let go of them and, as their bodies began to fall to the earth, they seemed to freeze in time for a split second. Then, suddenly, following their descent, Telok could hear their breath rush out, followed by deep groans. The last man in front of Telok turned to rush him. Telok struck the man just below the breastbone, taking all of his wind. As the man bent over, Telok lifted his knee and hit the man's forehead, lifting the man back to a standing position. Telok spun to his right, hitting the man with his elbow on the side of his jaw. The man's entire body lifted off the ground, and as he hit, it was evident he was unconscious. Telok immediately took a stance for another attacker, but there were none.

Korah had noticed Salmon, only because he recognized him from the other day. Korah was not expecting Telok or the other one who fought with him. In all of his rage toward Acts, he had blinded himself to the others. Korah raised himself up and now stood over Klee, Acts nearby, but on his knees. Korah considered his options to finish off Acts but waited to see what Abiram had planned.

When Acts stood, Abiram realized he had not considered the possibility of this young warrior taking a hit and recovering so quickly. He found himself in front of Acts without his arms raised for guard. Acts quickly advanced to Abiram and shoved the heel of his palm upwards, underneath the man's chin. His head snapped back, and he fell to the ground, also unconscious.

Korah knew he had a decision to make. If he tried to harm Klee, it would draw Acts into him, but if he went for Acts now while his back was turned, he could strike another blow to the back of Acts' head. He chose the latter, which dropped Acts back to his knees and then onto his side. Acts felt his body fall so slowly the entire day passed in his mind, stopping at the point he hit the ground. As Acts fell out of the way, Joshua's face became very clear to Korah. Anger flooded Korah's widened eyes. "You!"

Acts used his last bit of strength to roll on his back as Joshua jumped over him, grabbed Korah by the cloak, and flipped him over his shoulder. Korah hit the ground hard. Joshua looked at Acts and then to Klee, his anger building. As Korah rose to his feet, Joshua stepped in closer, punched Korah in the stomach, and doubled him over. Joshua raised his arm to forcefully bring his elbow to Korah's spine, but felt an unyielding force holding his wrist, preventing the strike. "They are finished, my Captain," Telok said softly behind him. "They are finished."

Joshua looked at Telok with wild eyes, but the calmness in Telok's face drained the anger, and Joshua started to breathe deeply, clearing his head. He looked, first at Salmon, then down to Acts' still form, and finally to Klee. As he moved quickly to Acts and gently began checking him over to make sure he was breathing, Salmon went to Klee and took the rope from her wrists. Acts was breathing but did not awaken. Joshua looked up to see Klee running to Acts' side. "Are you… alright, Klee?"

"Yes," Klee answered.

Telok and Salmon stood guard over them as they checked each other for wounds. None of the men they had fought wanted anymore. Those that could were running off into the sea of people, holding what hurt most in their bodies. It amazed Telok that not one of the people walking around them even noticed the scuffle. They seemed to be caught up in their own lives. The whole scene had only taken a minute, but it seemed so much longer.

Acts opened his eyes as Klee moved him gently, where she could see the blood coming from the back of his head. He made an effort to stand, but lost strength. Klee told him to stay down, but Acts showed no signs of comprehending what she was saying. Telok reached out and took him, lifting the unconscious Acts into his arms as if he were a small child.

Each man turned to see two men still on the ground and Korah on his hands and knees. He looked up to see Joshua staring at him. Korah winced slightly, the silence of the message shouting louder than any voice. Joshua fully intended to end Korah's life, but he was spared because of Joshua's friend—an Egyptian. Joshua turned his back to Korah and said to Telok, "Let's get back to my clan."

Telok carried Acts in his strong arms as they started to move back to Joshua's clan. But before going, Joshua walked over to Korah, bending down to jerk Korah's face to meet his. "You will not survive if you try this again."

The intensity in Joshua's voice and face caused alarm to rush over Korah. He said nothing in return, fearing he would release more of Joshua's deep-seated anger.

Once away from the area, Telok set Acts down. He had not awoken. Blood seeped from a gash in the back of Acts' head. Klee immediately began shouting orders. "Salmon, go get water. Joshua, we need some salt. And—" she looked at Telok and realized she did not know him, but there would be time for introductions and explanations later, "—you go get some cloth, as soft as you can find. We must stop this bleeding and get this wound closed."

At once each man hurried to find the things Klee had sent them after. Salmon returned with the water first, and then Joshua came running back with the salt. "Where is…?" she paused, and Joshua filled in the blank. "Telok"

Klee looked at him and he said it again. "Telok…" Then it struck her that was his name, and she said, "Oh!" She paused slightly. "Well, where's Te—?"

"Here I am," he called.

Klee took the cloth and dipped it into the water. Pressing it hard against the wound, she held it for what seemed to be a long time to the others. As she released it, the water kept the blood from sticking to the cloth and made the cut visible. It was a clean and straight gash about two inches long. She took some salt, put it on the cloth, wrapped it around his head, and replaced her hand to keep pressure on the wound.

Joshua said, "I will get a cart. He can't walk." He departed in a hard run.

Salmon's eyes were wide and full of panic. "Is he going to be all right?"

Klee smiled at him, and in a calm and assuring way, said, "The Lord is watching over him. He will be fine." As the words left her lips, she glanced over at Telok, and he smiled, nodding his head encouragingly.

Not much time passed before Joshua returned with a straw-filled cart, while ten men from his clan, who needed no invitation, followed. They had been sent by his uncle to check on the situation.

It took an hour to stop the bleeding completely, and another hour elapsed before Acts finally opened his eyes. Klee studied his face.

"You are truly a man of courage. I thank you for coming to my aid and for being my brother."

Acts smiled at her weakly but did not speak.

The four warriors and Klee now traveled in the safety of Joshua's clan and feared nothing. The tribe was moving toward the mile marker and Joshua knew he must leave his companions to sound the signal for the tribe of Benjamin to start the turn, following Manasseh. He did not want to leave Acts and Klee. Joshua looked into Klee's eyes and said, with regret, "I will return as soon as I can."

She took him by the hand and smiled softly. "I will be waiting for you."

Joshua looked down at Acts and touched his shoulder. Neither said anything, but the silence told both all they needed to know.

Joshua turned to Salmon. "Salmon, you will come with me." He glanced to Telok. "I entrust the ones I love to you."

Telok smiled confidently. "Do not fear, my friend. I will be with them at all times. The Lord will be our protection."

Joshua put his hand on Salmon's shoulder. "I need you by my side. I know you want to stay, but Acts and Klee are in good hands, and I need you to watch my back."

Salmon looked at Acts with a questioning expression, and Acts in a very weak voice said, "You have your orders."

Salmon smiled and turned to follow Joshua. They quickly disappeared into the crowd.

Telok looked down at Acts. "You are a warrior just as Joshua is."

Acts closed his eyes to rest with his sister's hand on his forehead and the back of his head resting in her lap.

She looked at Telok with gratitude softening her features. "You said just what he needed to hear. Thank you."

CHAPTER 7

NO MORE TIME TO WASTE

JOSHUA AND SALMON RACED BACK to the rock with plenty of time before Manasseh completed the turn and were on their way to the mile marker. It was now going into evening. Korah and his bunch would be passing soon. He wondered if there would be any more trouble, and he was glad that Salmon was with him. Both of them were thinking about all that had happened and of the blows Acts had received to his head. Joshua looked over at Salmon and could see the worry in his eyes, so he decided to redirect their thoughts to the matters at hand.

As they talked, each began to relax and marvel at the number of people passing in front of them. Salmon could see the dust of the tribes who had already turned and also the sea of people approaching the huge rock on which they stood. While they spoke, Abiram passed them, his hand holding his right side. He briefly glanced up at Joshua and Salmon before turning his head and continued to walk. Dathan never even looked up. Korah, on the other hand, stopped to glare at Joshua, but Joshua returned the stare with an expressionless gaze. Korah's look lacked the challenge it once had, his pride tempered, but the intensity made his hatred quite clear. He could not deny Joshua's ability and place as a warrior, and Korah detested the respect Joshua had in being the "servant of Moses." Turning his head away, Korah followed after Abiram and Dathan. No one else noticed the silent exchange, each absorbed in their own duties.

After Korah and his followers had passed, both Joshua and Salmon relaxed completely. Salmon turned to Joshua and naively asked, "Why did Korah and his men act the way they did?"

Joshua thought for a moment and placed a hand on Salmon's shoulder. "Not everyone looks at this journey with their eyes on the wonders of the Lord Most High as we do," Joshua answered, his tone filled with disbelief that men could act unsuitably during such a wondrous time. "To them it is merely a way out of bondage. Korah, Dathan, and Abiram are hungry to be leaders, as are Nadab and Abihu. They are so eaten up with the desire to be recognized by other men, they are willing to do almost anything to make themselves look good and appear important. Unfortunately, there are men who will listen to them, and some who will follow."

Salmon's face grew sad for those misguided. "I feel sorry they are missing out on the wonders the Lord is performing before their very eyes." After a pause, Salmon commented with a light laugh, "Acts is always seeing the hand of God. He brings out a desire in my heart to know our Lord more deeply. I want to be able to look and see through His eyes and learn more of what is really going on around me."

Salmon looked up into Joshua's face and smiled. "You have shown me so much of how God can work through men like my father, Acts, and me."

"What do you mean?" Joshua asked.

"You planned how to line up the parts of each tribe to accomplish the turn and stay in the order in which we left Egypt. The task seemed overwhelming to me, but you... you were so confident as you gave the instructions."

Joshua laughed openly. "Confident on the outside, nervous on the inside. Actually, I took the plans Moses had given me and just passed that information on in a manner that could be understood and followed."

"And you did it," Salmon added brightly.

The banner was waved to Joshua that Manasseh had reached the marker, and the tribe of Benjamin was approaching with the tribal leader, Abidan positioned out in front of the center of the tribe. To Joshua's relief, there was a smile on the face of Abidan.

"It is very good to see a smiling face, even if it is yours," Joshua teased.

Abidan laughed and winked at Joshua. Joshua raised the ram's horn to his lips, sounded the signal, and the tribe of Benjamin began their turn. He turned to Salmon and said, "I think it would be a good time for you to learn some of the fighting skills. They are the moves I taught Acts, and maybe when you see him again, you can teach him a few things."

Salmon stood with excitement. "I'm ready!"

~

Meanwhile, Klee was very tenderly changing the bandage on Acts and trying to determine what else needed to be done. The cool water on the cloth seemed to be helping the swelling, and the cut had been pulled together with the pressure of Acts laying his head on his sister's lap. Acts would sleep for a while and wake up, only to return to slumber. He said very little. Telok walked closely and kept a small jug of water within reach for Klee. Her eyes began to well up with tears. Telok looked over and stated apologetically, "I haven't stopped to ask if you were hurt."

"My wrists hurt a little and my side is sore. I just don't understand why this had to happen. Acts is still young, and Korah is supposed to be an example of how to be a man. Why did he act like that?"

Telok spoke with a low, calm voice. "His kind only thinks of themselves and what they can get out of any situation, whether it is something material or some amount of glory. They only seek to gratify their desires. This is actually what pushed me to the God of Joshua. I saw a man who served his God with respect and honor and in obedience not only to Him, but also to the people who had enslaved him. I see two extremes: Korah's total selfishness and Joshua's total servanthood. But I understand that in such an immense number of people, there will always be a vast array of personalities."

Klee began to wipe the tears from her eyes, as if wiping away the tension of what had taken place that day. Telok continued, "Joshua is truly a man who knows the value of a family. He has come from a good home and has been taught well. I can understand why Moses would want to have a man like Joshua at his side."

She felt a slight blush rising as she thought about all the admirable traits of Joshua. Klee looked down to see the eyes of her brother looking into hers. "What are you grinning about?"

Acts smiled up into his sister's face. "I just like watching your face when you think about Joshua and what he means to you. It makes me feel good. Besides, you're so easy to read."

"Easy to read! What does that mean?" she sounded back.

"The way you look at him and the way he looks at you…it's written all over your faces." Acts was now beginning to act more like himself.

Klee arched an eyebrow at him. "Is it that noticeable?"

Acts grinned. Klee looked over to Telok, and he mimicked Acts' expression, confirming the love Klee and Joshua shared was indeed "that noticeable."

Klee gazed wistfully off into the distance, a smile tugging at the corners of her lips. "He makes it so easy."

Acts laughed, but just as quickly grabbed his head. "You make it pretty easy for him, too, but I don't think I should laugh anymore." He yawned and fought to say the next sentence before falling asleep at the end of it. "You should hear some of the things he says…"

"Really?" Klee said excitedly. "What does he say?" She looked down expecting Acts to answer, but she found him asleep again. She sighed. "Guess I'll find out later."

Dawn's fingers explored the edge of the horizon, and the pillar of fire faded to make room for the fast-growing pillar of cloud so the whole company could walk in its shadow. Joshua and Salmon watched as the tribe of Dan surrounded them, and Ahiezer, with raised hand, showed Joshua that his tribe was ready for the signal. Dan was one of the last three tribes that were counted as the rear guard for the company. Dan had 62,700 men counted of fighting age and it was the second largest tribe. It took all of the morning and well into the afternoon for them to reach the mile marker.

Asher's tribal leader, Pagiel, approached the rock. "Joshua, I had doubts about this plan of yours at first, but I have been set straight in my heart and mind that what you spoke was the truth. It would seem that the words the Lord spoke through Moses back in Egypt, the order of the tribes, and the plan He gave you has indeed made us free. I ask you to forgive my doubtfulness of you. We truly serve a real and mighty God who has shown Himself loving."

"Pagiel, you were forgiven in my heart before we left the meeting, for in your eyes I could see you were having the same battle I had to deal with in my own heart. Is your tribe ready to experience the truth happening right now in their lives represented in this turn to the east?"

"We are ready, and our faith grows each day as I send runners to every clan encouraging them to stay strong in the faith."

"I will let Salmon sound the signal."

In an instant state of fear, Salmon turned slowly to Joshua, and as his eyes met his captain's, Joshua said, "You are ready. Just do your best. Give all that is within you, and they will know it is time."

Salmon timidly took the horn from Joshua's hand. He stood for a moment, the shofar trembling in his hands. Salmon took a couple of deep breaths and raised the horn to his lips. The sound was weak at first, but as he felt each blast grow stronger, he gained more confidence, especially when the tribe of Dan shouted and began to turn.

He looked over at Joshua and smiled shyly. "I think I got the hang of it."

"You did just fine, little brother."

The turning of Asher took the rest of the day and into the evening.

It was the evening of the second day when Joshua and Salmon watched as the tribal leader of Naphtali walked to the rock. Joshua got down off the rock to give Ahira a warm greeting and some instructions. When the tribe has completed the second turn, the entire march will be stopped. They would take a day of rest for the company of tired people. Even though they had been walking for almost three and a half days, no one seemed to notice. That would give Joshua and Salmon plenty of time to get back to their tribe. Joshua turned and nodded at Salmon where he stood on the rock and Salmon sounded the signal, this time with much more confidence. Naphtali was the final tribe, so the sound of the horn meant Joshua and Salmon were released to go back to Klee, Acts, and Telok. The wait had been excruciating, but now they could start a slow pace to their family.

~

At the front of the company, Moses walked and talked with the Lord. "How can you bring more glory to Your name after what You did in Egypt? It would seem the people would believe to their very core you are The Great I AM."

The Lord was tender with Moses, as always, and explained, **"The people have seen my hand against the people of Egypt, for I desired greatly the separation of you from them. Now I am going to test the hearts of the children of Israel so they will know that I am their God, their Lord, and their future."**

Moses sighed. "I understand that within such a number of people, there are those who follow simply to escape the hand of slavery and have not believed in their heart about who You are. They walk in fear those plagues could happen again to them."

"They have seen My hand moving against the Egyptians, but do not see My heart moving among the people. I have reserved that for you, Moses, My servant. There are certain individuals who have the deep desire to know Me and My ways just as you. In time, as they learn from you and in seeing My hand move, they will come to understand more clearly My personality and

why I command obedience. They will come to understand that in obedience, there is freedom and safety."

Moses smiled. "Joshua?"

"Yes. He is the one I have chosen to stand with you. He, and those who stand with him." The Lord allowed Moses to think about what He had said before continuing. **"I will show you where to make camp at Pi Hahiroth. It has been three days since the turn to the east has begun. I want the people to rest for three whole days, and then I want you to go all of the way until I tell you to stop. You, Moses my servant, are blessed above all men in the mass of people, and I will speak with you, and you will speak to the people. In the coming days, the test of their hearts will need all the strength they have, because in this test, I will bring great glory to my name so they will know... I AM."**

Joshua and Salmon had stopped for only a few hours and awoke early with renewed excitement. "There are several miles between us and Klee and Acts," Joshua stated. "How long do you think it will take?"

Salmon was a bit surprised Joshua asked him, but he thought for a moment before replying, "No more than a couple of hours."

"That's what I thought, too." Joshua replied. "Is your skin full of water?"

"No."

"We will fill them at the first water cart we see." Joshua instructed.

Salmon stood. "Let's get going. I'm ready to see how Acts is doing, and I know you're ready to see Klee."

Joshua arched an eyebrow at his young companion. "Is it that evident?"

Salmon only smiled as they turned to find the nearest cart.

As they ran, Salmon began to notice small things the way Acts would see them. The water carts were beginning to run a little low, but the thirst of the people was slight. Salmon also noticed that no one dragged behind. Everyone was able to keep up with their tribe.

Either no one minded the travel, or they were not aware of the time or miles.

Salmon laughed inside. *'Maybe I'll get to share this with Acts before he observes it?'*

They reached the last of the tribe of Ephraim and began to walk and slow their breathing down. The faces around them were smiling, and the mood of the tribe was pleasant. They seemed to be focused on the freedom they were experiencing.

Joshua looked around and finally found his father's cart a small distance away. Klee and Telok were not visible. Joshua knew they were safe with his clan, but he still wondered at their whereabouts.

Joshua felt the heat from a body moving close to him, and he spun around with hands ready to fight, but the deep blue eyes looking at him totally disarmed him in an instant.

"Gotcha!" Klee grinned.

"Oh, you got me, all right," Joshua laughed, picking her up and holding her close. Putting her down, he asked, "How's Acts and where's Telok?"

"Acts is doing well," Klee answered. "His head still hurts some, but there is no more bleeding, and the cut has closed well. I needed some more water in the bucket I was using, so Telok went to retrieve some. He won't be gone long."

Salmon moved closer, and Klee held out her arms and gave him a big hug, whispering in his ear, "Thank you for what you did in my rescue and for bringing Joshua back to me."

He smiled and turned bright red. He looked to Joshua. "I'm going to go see Acts." Joshua gave a nod of agreement, and Salmon ran over to the cart carrying his friend. He approached the cart slowly, finding Acts lying there with his eyes open. Seeing Salmon, he smiled and said, "Have you noticed that no one has lagged behind?"

Salmon gave a half-smile and shook his head. "Well, that was what I was about to ask you." They both laughed, but Acts made an awful face. "I just can't laugh that hard yet."

Telok appeared out of the crowd and gave his greeting to Joshua. "Onward we go!"

~

The Lord spoke to Moses, **"It's good to see their hearts lifted up. I love to see my children notice what I do for them."**

Moses rejoiced with the Lord. He asked, "Do I need to send for Joshua now?"

The Lord laughed, **"No. Not just yet. He's taking care of what you told him when you said, 'you don't need to waste any more time.'"**

Moses began to laugh with the Lord and replied, "Well, I'm glad he listened."

"I am going to bless him and his family and all those who serve with him as he serves you and Me," the Lord responded.

All that Moses could say was what he had been saying for months: "Thank You."

~

On the beginning of the first day of rest, as the pillar of cloud began to appear, Joshua turned to Klee and said, "I have to run on ahead for a little while to see my dad and mom after I speak to Telok and Salmon. I won't be long, but I need to do some things while we are stopped to camp. I'll be back as soon as I can."

"But why are you going?"

"It is just something my dad required for me to do a long time ago." As he started to run, he held onto Klee's hand for as long as possible before letting go and speeding up. She smiled and called out, "Don't be long, okay?"

Joshua waved his hand and yelled, "I won't!" Almost tripping over the same little lamb that seemed to make standing in Joshua's way a favorite pastime.

As he ran to Telok, he said, "Will you come with me? Salmon, please stay here with Acts and Klee. We won't be long." And without any further explanation, the two men ran off.

Acts glanced over at Salmon. "Kind of mysterious, huh?" he questioned.

"Yes," Acts replied, staring where Joshua and Telok had disappeared out of view. "Do you think we should follow them?"

Salmon balked at Acts. "Do you want either of them to be mad at you? You heard what Joshua said, and besides, Klee would give you another cut on your head to match that one if you disobeyed her."

Acts nodded reluctantly. "You do have a point. We'd better just wait here for them to come back and Klee's permission for me to get up."

CHAPTER 8

BURDEN NOW BLESSING

As Telok and Joshua ran, Telok asked, "Where are we off to, my Captain?"

"I must first see my father, and then I must find Uebel."

"Oh!! Enough said."

Joshua looked over at his companion. "You'll be doing this someday," he said with a brotherly smile.

The two men ran toward the front of the tribe and found his father, Nun. It was a happy greeting as Joshua began to ask his father's counsel. "I want to ask for your permission to go to Klee's father and ask for her hand in marriage."

"What a stunning question!" His father exclaimed. He looked over at Joshua's mother and said, "Precious, did you hear that?"

She beamed at Joshua. "Yes! I did," she answered, and she moved over to where they stood. The look on her face showed no surprise at the question.

"Thanks, Mother, but seriously, I need to talk about how to ask her father, considering the type of man he is." A little bit of tension strained Joshua's voice.

Nun thought for a moment. "Uebel is a man who only thinks of the moment. He is greedy, but also lazy enough that he won't want

"

too much responsibility, so here's what I think you should do: take two of our donkeys, two goats and two sheep, male and female.

"Let Telok take the donkeys and the sheep and stay off to the side where Uebel can't see him. Approach her father alone with the goats, and this blanket draped over your arm." As he spoke, Joshua's mother brought one of the blankets she had made for this day. "This will show him you're not there to fight. Then pose the question. If he says he wants more payment than the blanket and the pair of goats, ask him if a pair of donkeys would be enough. That will probably be more than he wants to take care of, but if he wants more, offer the sheep. It doesn't matter if he wants more, because I have been planning for this a long time."

Joshua looked at his parents and really did not know what to say. Telok voiced a question so Joshua could gather his thoughts. "So, in the man's response to the question of payment, I will not make my presence known?"

"That's right, Telok. You just wait until Joshua hears the answer." Nun turned to his son and said, "Son, you are welcome to all that I have. Remember this: he will want all that he can get, but he will not want the responsibility of caring for it."

"Thank you, Father. I do appreciate all you and Mother do."

"We want the very best for you and Klee." His father smiled. Joshua's mother then put her arms around him, saying, "I have asked the Lord to do this, and now I see Him answering my prayer."

Telok followed Nun to gather what was needed. As they walked, Nun clapped a hand on Telok's back. "I'm glad you are with him, Telok. He's always held a high admiration of you."

"Thank you, sir."

"I don't think Uebel is dumb enough to try anything stupid with Joshua, but it is always prudent to be ready. The whole tribe is proud of Joshua and all that he does for Moses." He glanced over at the young new Hebrew. "You giving up your time to be here for him means a lot to me and his mother. I know you are someone on which he can rely. Our family is close, and his brothers and sisters are able to see the Lord's hand on Joshua without being jealous. They also understand the Lord is helping him to choose men to stand with him to help carry out the orders of Moses. At this time, you are now part of our family through his choice." Nun smiled at Telok. "I believe he has chosen well."

Telok mirrored Nun's expression. "Thank you, sir. Since the day I met Joshua and his family, I have wanted to share in this family in some way. Now it appears I will finally have my opportunity. My father believed I would serve with Joshua all along!"

The two men collected what Joshua would need while Joshua's mother spent some time with her son. Nun and Telok returned with the animals. Nun entered the tent and addressed his wife. "Precious, I guess we better let Joshua and Telok go."

"Son," she said, cupping Joshua's face in her hands as if he were a little boy, "be strong and have courage. The Lord cares about who we have as mates, and He's had this planned for a long time."

Joshua hugged his mother and walked out to meet Telok at the tent's entrance. After a small distance from the tent, Telok reached around his companion's shoulders and squeezed him. "You, my friend, are a blessed man."

Joshua laughed heartily. "This I know, Telok. This I know."

Telok and Joshua moved over to the edge of the tribe to find Klee's father. They were able to do so without Klee, Acts, or Salmon seeing them. They spotted Uebel hanging around the far back end of the tribe. Joshua leaned into Telok. "I guess you had better stay here while I approach him from the front. I don't think he'll look around."

"I don't either," said Telok. "This is a big thing, important, so... now would not be the time to choke."

Joshua looked over at him and arched an eyebrow. "Thanks," he said, sarcasm dripping off the word. "Thanks a lot. How observant of you."

Telok laughed and pushed Joshua in the direction he needed to go. This levity felt good to Joshua.

Uebel looked up and saw Joshua coming. He grunted and did not turn to face Joshua. "Well, if it's not the great teacher of my son. What do you want?"

Joshua could feel his muscles tighten, but he managed to keep a calm look and mannered tone. "I have come to ask you one question."

Uebel stopped moving. "Now, what would that question be? Wait, let me guess. You want to marry my daughter, right?"

Joshua seethed silently. *'Calm down and do it the way you were told'*, he advised himself. He straightened a bit more. "Yes, I would like to ask for your daughter's hand in marriage," Joshua managed to say, his tone more business-like than he would have preferred.

Uebel made eye contact. "What makes you think I would let her go and get married?"

"I… have payment for her and would like the opportunity to show you."

He hated talking about Klee as if she were an asset with which to be traded. Joshua almost choked on what he really wanted to say to her father, but he bit his tongue.

The mention of gifts seemed to snag the older man's attention and the expression on his face changed from scorn and loathing to one of shrewdness and greed. "Payment?" he said, rubbing his hands together. "Would it be those goats with you?"

"Yes," Joshua answered flatly."

"I don't think two goats will be enough."

"I also have this blanket." Joshua extended his hand.

"Yes, the blanket would come in handy. Bring them over and let me take a look."

Joshua slowly walked over to him, and Uebel moved around the goats and felt the blanket.

Joshua offered, "I will take good care of her, and—"

"I don't care what you do with her," Klee's father interrupted. "If you want me to give her to you, it will cost you." He paused to think. "A pair of donkeys will do."

"Then it is settled: two donkeys, the blanket, and a pair of goats."

"Yes, that is the payment," her father repeated gruffly.

Joshua raised his hand for Telok, and Telok approached from the side with the donkeys and sheep.

"Here is what you required," Joshua said respectfully. "I'll let you know when the ceremony will be."

"Don't bother. She's your burden now." Uebel turned his back on Joshua and saw the sheep the young man had brought with him. He grunted and turned from Joshua, muttering, "I should have asked for more." He took the ropes that led the animals with the blanket over his arm and moved away from Joshua, not saying anything else.

Joshua stared blankly at Uebel, wondering what had poisoned the man's view of life. *'What happened to make this man so angry and so hateful of his own children?'* Unable to come up with an answer of his own, Joshua turned and rejoined Telok.

They started on their way back to Joshua's father to return the sheep. He shook his head. "Can you believe that man?"

Telok shrugged. "What was his burden… is now your blessing."

Joshua nodded confidently. "And a blessed man I am."

Telok laughed and held his hands up in front of him. "Now hold on, Joshua. You haven't asked, and she hasn't said yes."

"That's right! What if she doesn't want to get married yet?" Concern crept in his voice.

~

Acts was beginning to feel better, but his head still ached at different times. He had been lying in the cart since the incident, and he wanted to get up to help take care of some of the chores.

"No!" Klee said fiercely, clearly aggravated after she heard Acts ask for the fifth time if he could help. "You are not getting up until the pain in your head goes away. Your eyes still have dark circles underneath them, and you still get dizzy when you stand. So, you might as well get comfortable, because you are staying right where you are for a little while longer."

Acts knew better than to argue with her anymore, so he did as she said. Salmon did his part in helping with the chores, keeping close to Klee and Acts. As he fed the little lamb and its mother, Salmon stated, "I wonder what we will do after you are well."

"What do you mean?" inquired Acts.

"Well, at some point, Joshua will have to go back to the front to meet with Moses. Do you think we will go with him?"

Acts sighed, hoping to catch his sister's attention. "*You* might get to go. I don't think Klee will let me."

"That's right!" She sang out from in front of the cart.

Salmon chuckled at the look on Acts' face.

Acts looked up to study the pillar of cloud above him. "I remember Joshua saying we would camp until Moses said it was time, somewhere between Migdol and the Red Sea."

"Yes," replied Salmon, "I just hope we get to go with him, because I sure would like to see Moses again. He hugs just like my dad."

"Yes," Acts echoed softly. "The run to the front will be hard—most of a day, at least."

Salmon stopped to think a moment before saying, "Yes, that would be a hard run. I might have to stay here and help Klee watch after you."

Acts gave his friend an incredulous look. "Klee doesn't need your help."

"Help doing what?" she asked as she came around the other side of the cart where she gave water to the ox that pulled them.

Joshua and Telok walked up to the opposite side of the cart, away from Klee to the great delight of the boys.

Acts sat up a little, which made his head throb. "Hey! Where did you guys go?"

"I had a couple of meetings," Joshua replied evasively. "Where's Klee?"

"Give her a yell and she'll answer you," directed Acts. He rolled his eyes. "Or I could get up. She always appears out of nowhere whenever I try to move."

"I will not yell for her like she's some servant," replied Joshua. "And as for you getting up, you better stay right where you are, or you'll be in real trouble, not only with her, but with me."

Acts sighed heavily and dropped back to the straw.

"You are absolutely right," Klee said as she appeared from the other side of the cart. "And it's a good thing you didn't yell for me like somebody else would." She cut a glance at Acts.

Acts suddenly found a knothole in the wood on the side of the cart very interesting.

Joshua smiled at Klee. "Would you mind taking a walk with me?"

"I'd love to," she responded. She took Joshua's arm and grinned at Salmon. "Now you're babysitting."

"Babysitting!?" Yelled Acts, almost coming out of the cart and grabbing his head simultaneously. But Klee and Joshua had already started walking off. Acts lay back down, his head throbbing irritatingly. He and Salmon looked at each other, then over at Telok. Telok shrugged his shoulders and moved around to the other side of the cart to check out the wheels and make sure the cart was holding up well on the journey.

Acts and Salmon watched him the whole way. Telok turned around to find both of the younger boys still staring at him. "What?"

"We thought you might fill us in on what's happening," Acts replied.

"Do you think I would steal my captain's thunder?" Telok said dramatically.

Acts arched an eyebrow, annoyed.

Telok looked from one face to the other. "What?!"

Acts looked at Salmon, then back at Telok. "They are talking about how long I will have to ride in this cart, aren't they?" Telok just glanced back at the two young warriors leaving them in a state of wonder.

~

Joshua and Klee walked silently, though not uncomfortably. Klee looked at Joshua, her face serious. "I don't know if I have thanked you for what you did in the incident the other day."

Joshua sighed. "I'm sorry you were used that way. I am amazed at the whole situation. I just don't understand some people." He paused a moment before continuing. "I can't wrap my mind around the thought of doing what Korah, Dathan, and Abiram did. And Aaron's sons, Nadab and Abihu, participating, too? I just can't get there." They walked a few moments and then Joshua commented about Acts, "I would have to say your brother was outstanding, though."

"How's that?" she asked.

"He kept his head and did a very good job of looking out for you and fighting off two grown men. When Korah threw you to the ground, I almost killed him where he stood."

She squeezed his arm. "I'm glad you didn't. I don't know how Moses would have taken that kind of news."

He smiled at her. "I'm glad I didn't, either."

Klee relaxed a little more on Joshua's arm. "So… where are we going?"

Joshua cleared his throat and proceeded to form the question he had waited so long to ask.

Joshua and Klee walked toward the direction of Joshua's parents, and even though they walked with thousands around them, they felt as if they were alone. Joshua stopped and turned her to him, taking her hands in his. He looked into those deep blue eyes and began, "I have known in my heart for a long time I wanted to do this, and I have fulfilled the obligation in respect to our families…" He trailed off, suddenly feeling very nervous and very young.

"What is it, Joshua?" Klee looked curiously into Joshua's eyes. He could tell that she suspected what he might be asking her, and the sparkle in her gaze betrayed her excitement.

Joshua gained strength from her anticipation. "Klee, I want to take care of you for the rest of your life. And the only way I can do that is for you to say yes… to say yes, you will marry me. Klee, will you be my wife?"

Klee beamed but did not answer immediately. "I want a 'yes' from you as well."

Joshua's eyebrows rose. "Oh?"

"I want you to be my husband. Joshua, will you be my husband?"

Joshua studied her and tilted his head. "Is… this the way it's supposed to go?"

"For us it is. Now answer my question."

"Klee, I want to be your husband."

She smiled and stroked his muscular arms in a manner like she would do in smoothing a wrinkle on his shirt. "Good. I want to be your wife and with that settled, we can go tell your mom and dad."

Even though Joshua knew what the answer would probably be, he asked his question anyway. "What about your father? Do you think he would want to know?"

Klee gave a sad smile to the man she loved. "You don't have to try and make it better. I know he doesn't want Acts or me. He ceased to be my father long ago. I have been waiting and hoping you would ask me to be your wife. Acts and I are our own family, and now that you have *finally* asked me, I have new parents."

"This all seems so natural. If I had known it would have been this easy, I would have done it long ago."

Klee laughed. "You're a boy. Sometimes it just takes time for the Lord to get His message through."

As they walked up to Joshua's father and mother, Nun looked up from his work and smiled. "Oh, look, Precious!" he exclaimed. "It's Klee and Josh!"

The combining of a family had begun. Joshua's mother took Klee and immediately began planning some things about the wedding, leaving Nun and Joshua to discuss timing.

"So, when do you think the wedding should be, Dad?" Joshua asked.

His father looked off thoughtfully. "I'm thinking… early next year."

"Early next year!?" Joshua yelped.

His dad laughed loudly at his son's response. "How about we talk to Moses about this?"

"That sounds much better," Joshua agreed, feeling a little shaky. "Can Moses perform the ceremony?"

"I don't think he would have it any other way, Josh." His father only referred to him as Josh in times that would be very sentimental to him. This always meant so much to Joshua, because it let him drift back to when he was young.

"I think you need to ask him when you and your men head back to the front to meet with him. He will really get much joy out of the fact you asked Klee to marry you and that she agreed." They both laughed and all of the while thought, "I hope it won't be too long."

CHAPTER 9

THE CLIMB TO MOSES

JOSHUA AND KLEE RETURNED TO Acts and the others ready to share the happy news of the upcoming wedding. As they walked up to the cart, they found Acts standing by the vehicle. Klee looked over at him and put her hands on her hips. "Who said you could get up?"

Acts stared at her, wide-eyed. "I didn't realize that I was up. In fact, my head doesn't even hurt." He reached back to touch the cut, but he could not find it.

Klee walked over and he bent his head down so she could see. Her mouth dropped open, and her eyes grew wide. "It… it's gone."

Joshua, Telok, and Salmon immediately rushed over to see, and in fact, the cut was completely healed.

They all exchanged glances before Salmon looked at Acts and said, "This is one miracle I get to see, and you don't."

Acts grinned. "And this is one miracle I get to experience, and you don't."

Salmon scratched his head. "I didn't think of that."

All five laughed and patted Acts on the back.

When the laughing slowed, Joshua addressed them, saying, "Aside from the Lord *healing*, Acts, He has also worked in my life, and *we* would like to share it with you. Klee and I are going to be married!"

The group burst into a flurry of congratulations and embraces. Acts held his sister and said, "I am so happy for you!"

She smiled back into her brother's eyes. "We have a new family, you and me. The Lord has truly blessed us."

"Yes… Yes, He has," Acts replied, his mind racing with joy. He would have Joshua for a brother-in-law and the captain he loved and followed. His sister would have the best husband found on the face of the earth.

~

News of the wedding soon passed through the clan and then the tribe. Joshua walked with Klee until the evening of the day of rest and as people of his clan met them, they hugged the young couple with happiness for both of them.

It was at this time Joshua felt in his heart he needed to return to Moses. Leaving Klee would be more difficult than before. He told Klee that he and his team must be on their way back to the front to meet with Moses.

Joshua stepped up to Klee and held her in his arms. "I can go to Moses knowing we will have each other with the Lord's blessing; you as my wife and me as your husband." He looked into her beautiful face. "I do love you and will take care of you. I'm sorry I have to leave like this."

At that point Klee put her hand gently on his mouth, saying, "You are the servant of Moses, the servant of the Lord Most High, and I expect you to act like it. I will miss you, but I also understand you have been called to serve."

Joshua gave her one last squeeze before he turned to his men. "We must start to the front to meet with Moses. Fill your skins with water and grab some bread and fruit."

Each man began doing as ordered, and before long, they were ready to go. The distance they had to travel was only little more than a day's hard run. Ephraim was in the middle of the company. With one last look at Klee, Joshua turned to begin the run.

Acts quickly whispered to his sister, "If you see Janue, tell her I said hello."

Klee smiled and gave him a sisterly slap to the cheek. "I will tell them that two *courageous* men say hello. Now get going."

Acts made a face at his sister's sarcasm before laughing and moving to run with Salmon.

Salmon glanced at his companion. "Did you tell her?"

Acts grinned. "It's all taken care of."

Telok turned to watch the two catch up and said, "I guess you boys are set."

They could only smile.

~

As the four of them approached Moses, his greeting lifted their spirits, as always. Acts felt he would burst, waiting to tell Moses of his healing.

Moses smiled at the young boy. "The Lord told me that He would take care of you, and this only confirms His love for you." Moses turned his attention to the new member of the platoon that Joshua led.

"And who is this fine-looking warrior?"

Joshua answered, "This is Telok, a man whom I knew in Egypt. He is also a trusted friend. I trained with him in the imperial guard of Pharaoh."

Moses understood the type of discipline and character the man before him possessed, for Moses grew up training with the guards, and later in his life, he began to actually instruct those who protected his adopted grandfather, the Pharaoh. He took a moment to look into the eyes of the Egyptian, and after a moment of scrutiny, announced, "I remember meeting you in the palace. And I see, in the eyes of the man before me, a *new Hebrew*."

Telok's chiseled face spilt in a boyish grin.

Moses patted the olive-skinned shoulder as he continued to speak. "Joshua c-counts you as a good friend. I, too, will enjoy getting to know you as my friend."

Telok felt a deeper respect for Moses blossom in his heart. He now saw, not just a great leader, but the humble man who thought himself no more important than the youngest child. "What a privilege to serve someone so meek in spirit and strong in character!" Telok thought.

"Now that we have had a day to rest, it is time to begin the walk to Pi Hahiroth. It will be handled in the same way as when we left Egypt, with the exception of conflict with certain members of the tribe of Levi." Moses arched an eyebrow and smiled wryly at the young men around him. "I do not believe the last m-meeting has been forgotten."

They grinned sheepishly.

Moses continued "The Lord has made me aware of great things that are going to take place. Wonderful things. I have not been told every detail as yet from the Lord, but He is going to make a Name for Himself that will be known throughout the world." He turned his gaze to Acts. "You, Acts—the Acts of good will—may have already envisioned some of what may happen."

Acts looked back into the eyes of this humble man, and he could only nod his head in agreement, he had a mouth full of water.

"Call the runners and give this message: The specific signal we have used to get the entire company on the move from Egypt, will be given day in the morning. Take this time to get ready!" Moses looked into the deep, emerald-green eyes of Joshua to make sure he understood and made the comment, "Your children with Klee are going to have captivating eyes."

Joshua smiled. "Will you do us the honor of performing the ceremony?"

"I wouldn't miss it." Moses smiled as he turned to the rest and said, "We will begin the walk to Migdol. So, get your rest and fill up on fruits and vegetables. I want each of you ready, and I want you to know how much I love you."

The next morning Moses gave instructions as to what was going to happen. "The Lord has shown me where we are to camp in the region of two large hills near Pi Hahiroth. I want everyone ready to step off by mid-morning. Between those large hills is a saddle that leads to the valley. It is a couple of miles down to the shore of the Red Sea. The valley has enough area for the entire company of the children of Israel to gather. The first tribe will enter the valley, to be seated facing the shore. The company will enter the valley between the two hills which gently slopes to the shore. We will fill the valley like we would the colosseum, Front row first. Judah will pull into the valley and move all of the way to the south end of the open area. Issachar will pull in next to Judah and so on. The following tribes will fill in behind them the same way. There is a tall, watch tower that stands at Migdol. It is almost in the middle of the area, n-next to the shore. With the gradual slope from the hills to the shore, everyone will be able to see me. At the s-sound of the ram's horn everyone will stop what they are doing and face the tower on which I will stand. Not a man or woman will speak a word at the sound of the signal. There must be complete silence. I will address the entire company of Israel once the Lord tells me what to do. Are there any questions?"

They exchanged glances and confirmed they understood. "This is going to be a time of great glory. Be strong and courageous and walk in faith." Moses looked at his men, "Lord, you have surrounded me with faithful men." He smiled as he watched Joshua's mind begin to work.

Joshua thought for a moment, rubbing the back of his neck, before turning to Telok, Acts, and Salmon to give orders. "The 'orders for silence' is very important or Moses would have not mentioned it the way he did. Before the company pulls out, Telok and Salmon will leave after we eat breakfast. Make sure every runner has the instructions. I would like to have you back here before we step off. If something comes up and you will be a little late, you will have to do some running, if you don't make it back before we step off. That is why Acts will stay with me; encase you are late. I will need all of you once we reach the valley." Joshua paused to make sure they were following him. "If the people ask what we are going to do after we reach the valley, tell them Moses will receive orders from the Lord in what to do. That should satisfy who asks. Get word to Aaron that Moses wants him, with him. After we give the signal, we will move with Moses until we reach the valley." Joshua paused again to make sure his men understood. "Are there any questions? Good! Let's go eat!" Joshua turned to Moses, "Are you coming to eat with us?"

Moses laughed, "Well, of course."

~

After breakfast Telok and Salmon took off to deliver the plans. Joshua looked over at Acts and said, "Let's check on the people around us and make sure they get help if they need it."

Acts replied, "That is a good idea."

The visit was good, and Klee was enjoying getting to know Telok better. "You were in the same unit as Joshua in Egypt?"

"I was new and didn't really know anybody and one of the instructors pointed at me and to Joshua and said, we would train together. I immediately liked him. He was powerful and dangerous, but at the same time, power under control. He taught me to the point we started learning together. Both of us became instructors and soon I was an officer in the guard at the palace."

"What did he teach you?" She asked.

"He taught me battle moves and how to stay alive, but more than that, he taught me of the Lord and the promise he made to Abraham. What I saw in Joshua, I wanted in me."

"That is so neat. And none of it was ever a mistake. The Lord put you together so that, you would come to know the Lord. He is truly amazing."

"Yes! He is!" Telok replied.

They finished with the carts and eating. "We are gonna head out. The meal was great." Telok said, looking over at Salmon as he filled his mouth again.

He smiled with food showing around his teeth, "It tastes great, sis!"

She laughed at him and gave them both a hug."

The boys waved and off they went. "Man…" Salmon said with a sigh.

"What are you thinking?" Telok asked."

"I was thinking how blessed Joshua is!"

Telok smiled, "What do you mean?"

Salmon rubbed his belly and replied, "That woman can cook!"

Now Telok understood. "Yes! She can cook. And if we weren't getting all this exercise, we would be huge."

As they made their way through the tribes Salmon had a thought and he asked, "Telok, sometimes when I give orders, especially older people, I don't feel very strong."

Telok understood what he was trying to ask, "Salmon had not yet realized the authority in which he spoke. It was not by his authority he gave the orders, but from the chain of command to which he was connected. However, he was still very timid in giving older men orders, and Telok could see the battle in his friend's heart. He walked over and placed a hand on Salmon's shoulder. "In serving, there is always a chain of command, and in that line of authority, there is the recognition of who gives the orders. You have already established you serve Joshua, the servant of Moses, who is the servant of the Lord God. You don't have to explain your position; the Lord has already made your position clear to those around you."

Salmon nodded and said, "That makes good sense. Thank you."

"No worries." Telok replied.

The entire camp was ready to pull out. People were excited about moving again and toward the Land of Promise. Acts and Salmon sounded the signal, and it was echoed back all the way through the tribes. With a great shout, the walk began. Moses had his men with him and Aaron was at his side as well. The pillar of cloud was giving shade to the entire company and Acts looked at it and said, "I love the way the Lord takes care of every detail."

Salmon looked over at him, "What have you seen?"

Acts thought a moment and said, "We have seen 10 plagues, we have a pillar of cloud to lead and protect us by day and a pillar of fire to help keep us warm and give us light at night. He is a wonderful God."

Moses looked at Acts, "That is some good observation, Acts. Moses began looking around and asked, "Acts? Have you seen my staff?"

Looking around Acts spotted the staff and handed it to Moses. "Thank you!"

Moses held it out for Acts and Salmon to examine it. Moses began to teach them. "I have carved the highlights of my life and history of the Hebrews. The first thing is the calling, The Burning Bush. Next are the nine plagues."

Acts and Salmon inspected the carvings. Moses was very good at this. The pictures were easy to recognize.

Moses continued, "This is the last plague, Pass Over."

Acts looked up at Moses and smiled, "Hey – You have the Snake Mist on it!"

"I had to p-put that in, because you have seen it." Moses said with a smile. "The last thing I have is the turn."

Acts and Salmon complemented him on his ability. "So, what do you think will be the next thing? Those are all pretty big things." Salmon asked.

"That is something we will experience together." Moses replied and then he asked Acts, "What do you remember about the last vision?"

Acts thought a moment, "There was a dust storm with the sound of battle in it. There was deep blue water on the opposite side of the battle sounds. The Snake Mist showed up and fear began to grow in my heart. Even as the fear began to build, I was calmed by a man. He put His hand on my shoulder, and I could see a scar in His hand. It went all of the way through. I also saw scars in his feet that were the same. His countenance was demanding. He made the Snake Mist leave. He just pointed to the ground and the snake mist did what he said. I call the man, The Warrior of the Lord. He commanded everything. That is all I remember at this time."

"I'm gonna think on this a while. It is very interesting." Moses said.

They all fell back in step and just listened to the sound of their walk. Moses would turn around every once-in-while to check the tribes he could see.

They walked for one day and one night back to Pi-Hahiroth where the Lord showed Moses exactly where the valley was at Migdol. As they approached the valley, they could see that they were two to three miles from the shoreline of the Red Sea.

Joshua told his men to each grab a banner and they spaced themselves out. Joshua and Telok were in the saddle, between the two hills, which is where the tribes will enter. Salmon was halfway down the slope, and he would show the tribes where Acts was pointing. The company could see the Red Sea, but it was still two to three miles to the edge of the water.

Nahshon and the first tribe, approached Joshua and Telok in the morning. As the tribe passed through the saddle and were walking to the shore, Joshua could see they were a bit confused. They kept the tribe moving and did not allow people to ask questions or stop to talk.

By midday, there were four tribes facing the sea and the tower of Migdol in front of them. The tribe of Ephriam was approaching Joshua and Telok and they were ready to see Klee and Joshua's parents. The tribe was shown where to fall in, behind Issachar and Zebulun. Almost, right in front of the Tower of Migdol, where Moses would stand to address the company.

"It is good to see you!" Klee whispered to Joshua.

"It is more than good to see you, my bride to be." Joshua held her tight and squeezed all the stress and walk of the day out. "I have to stay here but Acts is…" Pointing to the tower, "He is right in front of the tower. That is where Ephriam will sit. I will see you when I can. I don't really know what's going to happen."

She stroked his back and said, "Moses will tell you what to do. You are doing just what the Lord wants you to do. And I am so proud of you."

She smiled and continued walking with Nun and his family. She said a quick, "thank you" to the Lord for her new family.

It took the rest of the day to get the other five tribes in place. Joshua and his men were now at the very back of the company, standing on the side of the south hill. They could see the entire company of people, animals and wagons and carts.

Acts was the first to speak, "I don't think I have seen the company all together like this. That is a lot of people and stuff."

"I didn't realize there was that much to move." Salmon commented.

Joshua looked at Moses and said, "We have to make it to Moses, and we will walk right down the middle of the tribes, straight to him. He smiled at his men and said, "Let's move."

As they walked down through the tribes, several people shook their hands, some would want to ask a question and some just wanted the opportunity to pat them on the back. As they walked up to Moses and Aaron, they each got a hug from both of them.

Moses said, "Have you ever seen anything like this? We have a lot of people!"

It was good to see Moses excited. "Will you sound the signal for everyone to be silent?"

"Yes, sir." Joshua turned and gave two horns to Acts and Salmon. "Sound the signal."

With clarity and volume, the sound went out and within a few minutes everyone was silent. The only sound was the wind, and the animals. Moses looked out across the people and as he began to speak, two wonderful miracles occurred; Everyone could hear Moses as if he was standing next to them. The second miracle was they could see his facial expressions and hand gestures.

All four of Moses men sat down, and each took a skin of water and a deep, long drink and a little time to relax.

CHAPTER 10

WALLS OF WATER

As Moses stepped to the edge of the tower to address the people, it appeared to Acts, Moses was standing in mid-air. He laughed and pointed it out to Salmon.

"It sure does look like he is just standing in the air!" Salmon replied.

Moses looked down upon the mass of humanity with the compassion of a shepherd looking at his flock, and he began to speak.

"Children of Israel!"

It was at this moment the people realized Moses neither shouted, nor raised his voice. It was as if he was talking to someone standing next to him, and every person in the large collection of people below heard him.

Moses continued. "It is by the blood of a lamb that we stand here today. The sacrificed lamb provided the sign of 'pass over' so the Destroyer could not touch those protected by the blood of the lamb. And in eating the lamb, it provided the strength to leave the p-place of bondage."

Moses turned to Aaron, and he began to speak, "The Lord Most High has given freedom to His chosen people, born from the promise to Abraham and passed down through Isaac to Jacob and finally through Joseph, who saved the family and the entire world at that time from famine. We have seen His mighty hand move in the ten plagues brought upon Pharaoh and Egypt. It is the Lord Most High who has brought us to this place, led by the pillar of cloud by day and the pillar of fire by night."

Moses spoke again. "The Lord God has brought us to this p-place so we may see His mighty hand move on behalf of His children. He gave me the instructions to bring you here so He can show you that, what is behind you… shall be gone forever."

There was a shout raised from the people that sounded like thunder. The praise lasted for a while. The people were thinking they would not see the Egyptians again because they would never return. But that was not what Moses meant.

Moses held out his hand to calm the crowd, and again the silence fell.

"I did not choose to be the man to go to Pharaoh, nor did Aaron choose. But the Lord chose us to go and speak for you. You did not choose yourselves to be the Children of God, but He chose you, and He is extending His invitation to you. It is an invitation to live a life worthy of Him. It is by the blood of the lamb and the word of your testimony that you live and follow after Him."

Moses continued. "The Lord did not yet reveal to me His exact plan, but I do know this." Moses paused for a moment and looked from one side of the camp to the other. "I know He loves you. He loves and cares for you far beyond what you can imagine. He has proven His love by what He has done and what He will do. You only need to obey."

Just as Moses finished his last sentence, a disturbance began from the top of the saddle between the western hills. A man came down the hill between the tribes of Naphtali and Asher, shouting as he ran. The people standing close to the top turned to see the commotion. "The Egyptians are COMING!"

Some of the men ran to the top of the hill to see for themselves what this man was screaming about and, reaching the top, they witnessed hundreds of chariots and thousands of soldiers racing toward them. The Egyptians were indeed coming, and they were marching straight for the Israelites. Though a long distance stretched between the Egyptians and the people of Israel, the men could see them clearly, for the Lord granted them vision to see their enemy approaching.

In one moment, mass hysteria broke out. Mothers began picking up their children, and people began to run about wildly, when suddenly they all heard the sound of the four horns. As the silence began to fall, one man's voice stayed elevated: Korah's.

His voice was clear as if the Lord *wanted* the man to be heard. "Was it because there were not enough graves in Egypt you brought us to the desert to die? What have you done to us by bringing us out of Egypt? Didn't we say to you in Egypt, 'Leave us alone; let us serve the Egyptians?' It would have been better for us to serve the Egyptians than to die in the desert!"

All at once, most of the people agreed with Korah and began shouting at Moses. Moses only raised his hands and said, "Do not be afraid! Stand firm and you will see the deliverance the Lord will bring you today. The Egyptians you see today you will never see again. The Lord will fight for you; you need only to be still."

The sound of his voice was almost too much for the people to take as their hands covered their ears, but they stilled and became quiet.

At that very moment, the pillar of fire descended on Moses. Acts looked into the pillar, as did the others, and could barely make out Moses' body. They heard a sound like nothing they had ever heard, and for a few terrifying moments, they thought Moses would be consumed.

Inside the pillar of fire, Moses had communion with the Lord, and He reproved Moses, **"Why are you crying to Me? Tell the Israelites to gather all that belongs to them and to move. Raise your staff and stretch out your hand over the sea to divide the water so that the Israelites can go through the sea on dry ground. I will harden the hearts of the Egyptians so that they will go in after them. And I will gain glory through Pharaoh and all his army,**

through his chariots and his horsemen. The Egyptians will know that I am the Lord."

The Warrior of the Lord, who had been traveling in front of Israel's army, withdrew and went behind them. The pillar of cloud also moved from the front and joined its fiery twin, forming a barrier between the armies of Egypt and Israel. The communion with Moses only lasted a few moments, and then Moses could be seen once more after being covered in the pillar.

Moses understood the Lord would give the children of Israel time to obey, but they must begin to move in an act of obedience.

Moses motioned for Joshua, and Moses put his arm on his servant's shoulder. Acts, Salmon and Telok watched everything intently, and Acts began to pray in his heart:

'I have the wonderful opportunity to choose. It was You, O Lord, who chose this people to be known as 'the children of Israel,' and in that great number of people, You, chose me. You've given my sister and me a new family. You have put me under the teaching of Moses, your servant, and placed me in the service of Joshua, the servant of Moses. I have new friends and have seen wondrous things. How could I not want to follow wherever You lead? As Moses said, 'It doesn't matter how you feel, but whether you obey.' I choose today… to obey.'

Every person watched as the pillar of fire and cloud move like tornados to the back of the company. A wall formed between the Egyptians and the Hebrews.

As they watched, Acts covered his right ear and stumbled and fell to the ground. Joshua ran to his young friend's side, attracting the attention of Salmon, Aaron, and Telok.

~

In his mind, Acts saw a watery grave. Dead men floated on top and under the water, and more Egyptian surfacing from its depths. The snake of mist moved over the dead and seemed to be laughing. Acts felt as if he was lying in the bottom of the sea, and the mist looked at him, but did not approach. He struggled to move, but he felt so heavy. A hand came into focus, reaching for him, but the face was hidden from Acts. He did see the scars on the hands of the man. His clothes shone brilliantly white, so much so, that it forced Acts to look down, and when he did, he noticed the same type of scars on the man's feet as well: holes, all the way through His hands and feet. As he looked up again, he observed the man's side opened like a warrior in battle. Acts extended his hand to the man, and as he took hold of the stranger's grip, the hand turned into Moses', and the rest of the world came into focus.

It took a moment for Acts to realize his dream had ended. He saw all of his companions staring down at him. Salmon worried over him. "Are you alright?"

Acts held up his hand to quiet Salmon. Moses gave Acts a moment and then asked him, "Acts, was it like the others?"

"No, it was different from the others."

Moses asked, "Acts, were you afraid?"

Acts thought a moment. "No, sir," he answered. "Not this time. I wasn't alone. The snake mist was there looking at me, but there was also a man with terrible scars on his hands and feet and a wound in his side. He was so bright I couldn't look at his face, but I felt no fear of him. I saw in the sea, the living in the process of dying and the already dead." Acts scrunched his face in concentration. "It's hard to see it now."

Moses patted Acts on the shoulder. "That's fine, Acts. You've done well with all that you have seen. You and I will talk about all this very soon. Now, do you feel strong enough to complete the mission?"

"Yes, sir. I'm fine now."

Moses turned to speak to the people again. The movement of the pillar had completely silenced everyone, including Korah. Moses' voice rose as clear as before. "Each tribe will receive the signal to move, as before. We are to walk toward the Red Sea, and when we reach the shore, we are to keep going. We will advance on the sea as one people. My men will be in the very back of the company. No one is to be behind them. I will be at the very front. The Lord is moving on our behalf, and I am giving these instructions directly to you, now."

Moses did not tell them the Lord would divide the waters. They were to approach the sea in faith. As Joshua was giving the orders, Moses turned to face the Red Sea, and raising his staff over the sea for the company of Israel to see, a mighty wind began to blow. It blew with such force that walking into it became difficult. After Moses raised his staff and the wind started its journey across the water, he turned to Joshua and said, "Let's go. I will lead Judah toward the shoreline and then into the sea."

Joshua looked back at Moses and Moses put his hand on Joshua's shoulder, saying, "It will be absolutely fine. You and your men just keep the p-people moving. Some of the people may want to stop, but don't let them. It is going to be glorious!"

After coming down from the tower, Aaron bid farewell to Moses so he could accompany his family and Miriam. Moses smiled at Joshua and turned to lead Judah toward the sea.

All night long, the tribe of Judah slowly moved toward the Red Sea, following Moses with the wind in their face. Keeping the animals moving and watching after the children and elderly was a big job for the tribes as they moved. Joshua's men sounded the signal for Issachar to follow, making sure they kept as close as possible to Judah.

As Moses kept a steady pace, Nahshon walked up beside him and asked, "Where are we going? The sea is in front of us and the Egyptians are behind us."

Moses reproved Nahshon and said, "It is not the sea in front of us, but the Lord." He smiled at Nahshon so he would know Moses was not chiding him like a child, but merely pointing out they walked by faith. Nahshon could not help but follow such faith in this man who led the children of Israel.

The Egyptians, on the other hand, were in complete darkness on the opposite side of the pillars of cloud and fire and could not see where to put their next step. With the wind blowing so hard, they could not hear what was happening in front of them. They were completely disabled and cast curses to the children of Israel. The men were frustrated, and, in that frustration, their fear mounted in their hearts. Not only fear, but rage began to build, a rage that overtook the fear.

Joshua and his squad faintly heard the Egyptians curse the Hebrews from behind the pillars of cloud and fire, and Acts glanced over at Telok to ask, "What does it feel like being a Hebrew?"

Telok considered the question a moment and answered, "I've lived in spiritual darkness all my life until I learned there is a God of light. He has proven Himself through the Passover and, in my father, Kemuel taking me into his home to save me from death. The Egyptians, on the other side of the pillars, not only walk in spiritual darkness, but physical darkness as well, and I can't praise the Lord enough for the freedom I have found through walking in His light."

Acts smiled at Telok's words, for hearing the word of his testimony, built faith in his own heart.

It was early morning, before light of the sun could be seen, the entire tribe of Judah had reached the shoreline, or where the shoreline should have been. Nahshon and his tribe were witnessing something that amazed and terrified them. Before them was a path that led down into the heart of the sea with a wall of water on the right and a wall of water on the left. It was a path wide enough to accommodate the largest tribe. The people looked but could not take in what their eyes were seeing. The path led down a long slope, around some small hills and large rocks, but for the most part, it was straight as far as they could see. Moses turned to Nahshon and laughed. "There is our God, Nahshon."

Nahshon could not take his eyes off the sight, and the only thing that made it past his lips were just a few words. "Can you... see...?"

Moses laughed at his lack of speech. Moses raised his staff, waved for them to follow him, and they started their descent down the slope. The water was at eye level and, as they walked, the walls of water began to stretch higher and higher until they could no longer see the top. The water on the surface to the right and left still had waves, but the path was dry all the way to where the dirt met the wall of water. The path was huge as the people descended down into the heart of the sea.

Judah was three miles into the path and each person began to see the miracle for themselves, the reactions were all the same. The amount of distance was closer between the tribes than in the march to Pi Hahiroth.

One by one, the people walked onto the sea floor. When the final tribe of Naphtali passed the squad of Joshua's warriors, Acts noticed that the silence on the shore hurt his ears. He asked the men with him, "Do you hear that?"

Each man stopped to listen, and after a moment, Salmon responded, "I don't hear a thing."

"Exactly," replied Acts.

Telok nodded, gazing around with calculating eyes, his defenses raised. "No birds, cattle or any animal."

"Not even a baby crying." Acts added.

They realized another miracle of the Lord filled their midst. The army who wanted them dead had no idea of what was happening in the light, even with the mighty wind silenced.

Moses was about twelve miles into the path of the sea when he climbed up onto a very large rock, scaling it like a young man. He turned to see the children of Israel coming toward him. The pace moved quickly, but people still took the time to look up at the walls of water. They were perfectly smooth and had a beautiful shade of blue green. Inside the wall of water, they could see movement of the creatures who lived there. The march of the people's feet and the squeak of the carts being pulled echoed softly between the barriers but did not travel past the shoreline. Not one person said anything louder than a whisper. Nahshon walked up to Moses and said softly, "I am asking you to forgive me for doubting the Lord and you. I could have never dreamed of such a thing."

Moses smiled. "To tell you the truth, neither could I."

~

Over half the tribes had reached the bottom of the valley floor of the sea. Joshua and his squad stood looking at the people. Telok looked over to Acts just as Acts cupped his right ear, and Telok caught the boy in strong arms and lowered him to the ground.

Acts could see, in his dream, events that were actually happening and also see in the spiritual realm.

Angels surrounded the children of Israel in the sea, watching and protecting. In the vision, Acts turned his head to look into the darkness in which the Egyptians stood. The snake of mist was moving over them as if he were counting the souls it would take. It jerked its head to look Acts in the eyes, but it could not approach him, the snake of mist looked above Acts and showed great fear. Acts looked to see what it was, and there was the same man that was in the last dream. As the snake of mist concentrated on the Egyptian army, it laughed wickedly, but when it looked at Acts, it cringed with fear and torment.

Acts felt cool water on his head as he opened his eyes, and his three companions came into focus. He blinked several times and heard Joshua. "You're alright. Telok caught you and it only lasted a minute." To Acts it seemed much longer.

They let him regain his composure and take a drink of water before asking him questions.

Acts was slow in coming back to reality, and as he did, he tried to explain what he had seen. It was difficult for them to picture in their minds what he described, but they did not press any further. They raised him to his feet and Joshua steadied him. "Are you ready to start the walk into what you have seen?"

Acts rubbed his temples. "The man. The same man with the scars was there protecting me. I felt no fear, nor did I feel defenseless."

As they walked past where the shoreline should've been, they took one last opportunity to listen to the army that pursued them. Joshua shook his head. "What we see and hear today we will never experience again."

They all exchanged glances and Salmon said, "Down we go."

The walk began, and the pace was fast, because they were going downhill into the heart of the sea, following Ahira and his tribe of Naphtali. It had taken all day for the last tribe to make it to the flat level floor of the sea, and now the children of Israel were in line and on somewhat level ground. Moses could see the slope of the other side rise and knew it would be a difficult walk. If anyone was going to stop and rest, it would be there. He suddenly realized, *'With Joshua and his squad in the rear, no one will want to stop.'*

~

Behind the pillar of cloud, the Egyptians were now thrown into a situation in which all they could do was wait. It was so dark that not one man could see where to put a step. Some of them began to doubt, but there was nothing they could do except obey orders.

~

Telok's mind moved in and out of his past relational ties and where he stood now, in the presence of such an awesome God. He personally knew many of the soldiers that had been sent by Pharaoh, sent to kill the Hebrews and bring a large part of them back into slavery that would be much harsher than ever before. He did not understand how he could have been so blind for so long to this God he now knew intimately. *'Everywhere I look I see Your Hand'*, he prayed. *'In the air I breathe, the water I drink, plants, animals, and even in my own body and how wonderfully made it is. I have never known such peace.'*

Telok thought back to the time when he and Joshua trained and remembered Joshua to be genuinely concerned about the Egyptian's well-being. Even when Telok seemed depressed, Joshua noticed and made himself available if Telok needed to talk. In all of this, Telok now looked back and could see the Lord inviting him to be part of a new kind of freedom, a freedom that settled deep inside. He was an adopted Hebrew, and over the past several years, he came to know and love his adopted father, Kemuel. He kept his relationship with Kemuel a secret for obvious reasons concerning the Egyptians. If the Hebrews found out, they could have given away his relationship with his father and put them both in danger. Telok did not know what the future held for him, but he knew his future was in the hands of an awesome and powerful God.

~

As Acts and Telok moved behind the company, Acts was aware of his friend's silence. Acts left Telok to his contemplations, but after a while, he interrupted him. "What are you thinking about?"

Telok sighed and looked up at the walls on his left and right. He was in wonder of the Lord, how He led me to Joshua and my father, Kemuel. He hesitated before he commented about those on the other side of the darkness. "I know many of the soldiers on the other side of those pillars, and my heart aches that they have chosen to remain in darkness. But I know they had their choice, and I am grateful to the Lord for softening my heart the way He did."

Acts found himself enjoying the conversation with Telok. Suddenly, perceiving a blessing Acts was fairly sure no one had mentioned to his older friend, he said, "Telok, no one sees you as Egyptian. They see you as Hebrew, and not only as just another Hebrew, but as one who serves under Joshua and Moses. Everyone we've seen has respected you and treated you with admiration."

Telok thought about Acts' words. Telok had been so caught up in doing as Joshua had asked and was so involved in the family affairs of his new brothers, he had not noticed his acceptance. "You're right. Isn't it just like you to point out another one of your insights about our God? Thank you. That makes me feel even more a part of the family."

Telok noticed someone having difficulty while trying to pull some water out of one of the carts. He ran over to see what the problem was and noticed the levels were much, much lower than they had been the previous day.

He jogged back over to his group. "The water in that cart is almost gone. We must assume the other carts are in the same trouble."

Joshua sighed and pressed his lips together. "We should monitor the water so that we can tell Moses. I hope the Lord leads Moses to a water source soon." He thoughtfully added, "However, I do feel the Lord will supply one."

Telok smiled. "I do, too. I was just bringing it to your attention."

Acts grinned at the two older brothers as he heard Joshua say, "I'm glad you did."

Telok shrugged. "It never hurts to have a plan, plus Moses will want to know if he doesn't already."

Several miles in front of them, Moses had come across a large flat rock he climbed to stand on and once again looked back upon the people who followed him as he followed the Lord. The sight was spectacular, and Moses commented to the Lord, "I have noticed that water carts getting low."

Moses felt the Lord smile, and it soothed him. **"I will supply. You need not worry."**

~

Joshua had switched to soldier mode and noticed a no-way-out situation with the distance to the other side of the sea. Because of the walls of water on both sides, the Egyptians had a straight shot at the people if the pillars of fire and cloud ever vanished. Telok noticed the same thing, and he leaned into Joshua to express his concern.

Joshua looked at him and said, "Don't give up the faith my friend. He's still the Lord, even with the sea in front and the Egyptians in back."

Telok nodded. "You are right."

Moses spoke in his heart to God, "Lord! You have given me such wonderful men to work under my command. That Salmon is a real achiever."

"Yes, he is." There was a pause. **"Acts weighs on your heart."**

"Yes, Lord, he does. You have allowed the boy to see things that have not yet happened, things of which You have told me. I told him I would talk to him about them, but I don't know what to say."

"Acts is very sensitive to My Spirit. He is able to put preconceived ideas aside and allow me to speak to him. You will use him, Moses. He will be a servant to you and later to Joshua as well. I have wonderful things planned for him, Telok, and Salmon. A family, a place of service, and a relationship with me that will be much like yours. But to you, only, will I speak in this way, Moses, because you are My servant and My friend. I called you out of the desert and into My presence. You can tell Acts I will use him in serving you, and the things I tell him in dreams will be made known as he walks with Me. He need not ever fear. This is what you can share with Acts."

"Thank you, My Lord. You taught me well on the back side of the desert."

"You learned well," was the soft reply of the Lord.

~

Acts turned around to look at the pillars and was surprised to see only the pillar of fire. The pillar of cloud had moved back to the front, with it stretching over the company.

"The Lord is keeping them back with the pillar of fire," Telok commented. "They can see, but not advance. This only brings their fury to a greater level. When they are set free to attack, they will do so with all of their might."

Joshua looked ahead, climbed up onto a large rock to get a better look, and could see the path start upwards as it led out of the sea on a steep slope.

"Out of the great number of people, there are those who think the threat of the Egyptians is over and will want to slow their pace, maybe even stop. Moses told me we need to keep the people moving. Be ready. Let's spread out across the path."

~

Moses felt such compassion for the children of Israel. Nahshon walked up to him and asked, "Is there anything wrong?"

"No," Moses answered. "I was just taking in the sight of the greatest miracle I have ever heard of, with the exception of the ten plagues." This brought a chuckle from both of the men.

Nahshon's tribe had been granted the honor of carrying the bones of Joseph out of the land of slavery and into the land of his father. Nahshon commented, "We never can tell what the Lord will do. Just… never can tell."

Moses smiled at his statement, but in his heart the Lord spoke to him,

"They can see what I do, but you, Moses, will know *why*. You will know my personality more and more."

~

Klee, Janue, and Shade had been walking together since they entered the path. They communicated in glances. Each held a holy fear in their hearts, and Klee whispered a prayer the girls could hear. *"Oh, Lord, our God, please keep our boy's safe and let them make good time in reaching us again."*

Both of the girls smiled and continued the pace in keeping up with the tribe of Ephraim. They were beginning to feel the burn in their legs, but they would keep going.

CHAPTER 11

NAOON

T HE PEOPLE MOVED AT A good, strong pace, fear partly driving them in this awesome miracle. All of them marveled at how high the walls were from the valley floor to the top where sea level would be, if they were in a boat.

The men of Joshua began to spread out, Joshua standing in the middle, Telok to the south, and Acts and Salmon to the north with Acts walking next to the wall. Act began to inspect this miracle by looking at the ground and rock formations. These were things no man had ever seen. The colors in the rocks were so sharp and brilliant, polished by thousands of pounds of water and currents that had moved over them from the time the Lord spoke them into existence. He looked over into the wall of water itself and could see fish swimming right up next to him. *'I wonder if they are as surprised to see me as I am to see them,'* he thought, smiling to himself.

Acts saw all sizes of fish, but one in particular came up next to the wall and stared at him. Acts grinned. "Well, hello there, my fishy friend. I wonder what type of fish you are. You don't look scary." Acts walked closer, and its tail moved slowly back and forth. Acts held out his hand toward the fish, and it stayed put. Acts tilted his head to one side in wonder, and he slowly put his hand into the water toward the fish's head. The water was very cold, but Acts continued to reach into the water. He was pulling up his sleeve when the fish swam up to his hand and put its head underneath the hand of Acts. Acts blinked in surprised. He rubbed the fish's head like he would a puppy's and said, "Your skin is slick and smooth! You don't have any scales, either. I think I'll call you 'Smoothie.'"

Salmon turned his head to check on Acts and noticed that his friend's arm was stuck almost all the way into the wall of water. Alarmed, Salmon ran to where Acts stood. As he approached Acts, Salmon stopped running and looked in amazement.

"What… what are you doing?!"

Acts looked at him and back at the fish. "Come on over and meet Smoothie."

"Smoothie?" Salmon looked confused. "What's a Smoothie?"

"He's my new fish friend."

Salmon frowned. "Are you supposed to be doing that?!"

Acts shrugged. "I'm just exploring this wonderful miracle of the Lord God Almighty. And it is truly a wonderful miracle! Do you realize we are seeing things no man has ever seen? Look at these rocks - their color and the way they're shaped. No man has ever walked on rocks such as these."

Acts pulled out of his pocket five smooth stones of brilliant colors. He nodded to Smoothie. "Have you ever seen a fish like this one?"

"Well, no, come to think of it," Salmon answered. He studied the fish for a moment before he hesitantly asked, "Can I touch Smoothie?"

"Sure, he won't bite," Acts laughed, and just has Salmon's hand entered the water, Acts added, "I don't think he'll bite."

Salmon jerked his head to Acts, but he did not have time to react before Smoothie had already put his head under Salmon's hand. "Wow," Salmon remarked. "His skin is so…"

"Smooth?" Acts replied.

Salmon thought for a moment. "So, that's where you got it!"

Acts chuckled. "Come on; we've got work to do."

Salmon pulled his hand back out of the water. "See you around, Smoothie."

And with that, the fish swam off.

Salmon scratched his head, thinking, *'Not in a million dreams would I have thought such a thing possible.'*

~

Some time passed, and the people moved over a lot of ground, but the pace began to take its toll on the strength of many of the people. Joshua and his men had to really work to keep everyone moving. Some people wanted to sit down, and they were starting to complain about the speed.

"Can't you get Moses to slow down some?" an old man yelled.

Joshua said in a calm voice. "If this is the pace the Lord God gave to Moses, it is a pace everyone can keep. Rely on your Lord for strength and endurance. Just keep moving."

The old man said nothing more, but he turned and began to walk again.

A young mother had stopped in the back of the last tribe to breastfeed her newborn. She was sitting beside a rock. Joshua saw her and ran up to meet her.

"Are you, alright?" he asked.

"Yes," she replied. "My baby needs to eat again. I thought I could keep up with my tribe, but I keep losing ground every time she gets hungry."

"All right," said Joshua as he looked up to catch Telok's attention. "Can you get a cart and bring it over here for me?" Joshua shouted.

"Yes, sir," came Telok's reply.

After a few minutes, Telok provided a cart with a young man to lead the oxen pulling it.

"Here you are, my captain, and a fine young man volunteered to assist," Telok said.

"Thank you, Telok." Joshua focused on the young man in front of him. He was tall, lean, and strong in build. He looked to be about the same age as Acts and Salmon. "And thank you for your help. What is your name?"

"I am Guni, son of Jezer, of the tribe of Naphtali," he answered with boldness. The young man's presence was very positive, and Joshua and Telok both made note of him.

Joshua asked the young mother to ride in the cart. "Now you can make sure your daughter receives enough, and you won't have to worry about being left behind." He paused a moment before asking his next question. "Where is your husband?"

She looked down for a while, and when she lifted her head, Telok noticed the young woman's eyes and saw how beautiful she was. Her voice was soft. "He was killed in Egypt a couple of months before the baby was born."

"I'm sorry to hear that," Joshua replied gently. "Do you have anyone who is helping you with your belongings?"

"No. My belongings are on that ox over there," the young woman replied.

Telok stepped forward, and Joshua took the cue. "This is Telok. He is a very trusted friend and soldier. He will accompany you until you have reached the other side."

Telok studied the young woman with tender eyes, but his face was serious as he said, "I would be honored, my captain." He walked over and pulled the oxen carrying her belongings and tied it to the cart. "I will be close at hand and will probably be in your sight at all times," he told her. "If you need me, all you have to do is say my name."

The young woman nodded, and she stared curiously at Telok. "Are you Egyptian?" she asked shyly.

Telok and Joshua both noticed her tone, and Telok answered, "Yes."

"But - you are Hebrew now?"

"Yes."

She smiled and said, "I am glad for you. Thank you for this service. And thank you, Guni," she added.

The young man smiled, blushing slightly. "You're welcome."

"I must get back to my position," Joshua announced. "I know you're in good hands." He smiled at Telok and turned and ran back to the middle of the path.

Guni turned to Telok and said, "Whatever you need, sir, I will do."

Telok nodded. "Do you need to run and tell your family where you are so they won't worry?"

"No sir. That is my clan and my father just ahead. He's been watching, and I think he knows what's going on." The young man waved to his father. His father waved back, turned, and began walking again with his clan.

"Good. I will be right over here." Telok moved to leave and then realized he did not know the young lady's name. "What is your name?" he asked her, having trouble concentrating as he stared into the young woman's eyes.

"Naoon," she replied.

Telok stumbled in repeating her name, "Na-oon." After a moment of repeating the syllables, he finally put it together. "Naoon. That's a very pretty name."

She smiled. "I am a descendant of Serah, the daughter of Asher for whom our tribe is named."

"Then you shall be treated as a princess." Telok smiled and turned to go.

Guni said, as he and Naoon watched Telok walk away, "Telok has a reputation as one of the finest warriors in Egypt."

"Really?" asked Naoon, turning her eyes on Guni.

"Yes! He trained with Joshua for a long time, and he helped in the fight with Korah and his goons. Telok didn't even get a scratch. Three of my best friends are runners from the tribe of Ephraim and they told me all about it. In fact, one of them is in the same clan as Kemuel. Kemuel is Telok's new Hebrew father. That's how I know these things."

Naoon looked out and studied Telok's movements and interactions with other people. He was so polite. "He doesn't come off as someone with that type of reputation."

Guni shook his head. "Nope. I hope to train with him one day."

Naoon nodded slowly, her eyes still on Telok, curiously.

As Guni led the oxen, the baby began to suckle, and soon the steady pace and movement of the oxen put her sound asleep in her mother's arms, between walls of water. This would be something she would tell her grandchildren and great grandchildren.

Meanwhile, Salmon had run into several people who were seated in a group. Salmon walked up to them. "Can I help you in any way?"

"No, thank you," was the reply from a woman who appeared to be in her forties.

"Then may I ask why you have stopped?" Salmon asked.

"We need to rest for a while. We're tired, and we've been walking at this pace for a long time now," was the reply from another woman about the same age.

Salmon looked around at the four ladies and three men who seemed to be near the same age, but there was something about their attitudes that alerted Salmon on the inside.

Salmon kept his voice and manners calm. "I'm going to have to ask you to keep moving as Moses asked."

"Why would we want to do what *you* say?" sneered a man, speaking down to Salmon as he stood to his feet.

Salmon slowly and coolly turned and squared up to the man.

"The instructions, given by Moses, were passed to Joshua, the servant of Moses then provided to your tribal leader who shared them with you. They were to keep moving and to not stop."

Salmon never took his eyes off the man, showing he had no fear even though he was outnumbered.

The man crossed his arms defiantly. "We will start moving *after* we take some time to rest!"

Salmon stepped up to the man and looked him straight in the eye. "I am Salmon, the servant of Joshua, who is the servant of Moses. You will not talk down to me, and you will turn and start moving as you were instructed by Joshua right now."

The man seemed impressed with this young man's confidence, but he was not willing to back down just yet. The other men moved around Salmon to block him off. As the man that had been speaking stepped back, he bumped into someone. It was Acts.

Acts surveyed the situation dispassionately. "Is there a problem I can assist you with, sir?" he asked the man who had run into him.

The women began moving out of the way.

Neither Acts nor Salmon took their eyes off the man who had been speaking. This made him very uncomfortable, and just as he drew in a breath to say something, another voice spoke.

"I can see there is a problem here. No one is moving forward." Joshua stood with his arms crossed, expression unhappy. He met each man's glare without flinching. Without removing his gaze, he nodded toward his two younger companions. "This is Acts and Salmon, and they are under my command and speak with my authority. Now, if you three men want to take this to a physical level, then by all means, do your best. But I want you to know that I and the other man behind you have trained them."

The men whirled to see Telok standing there, their eyes full of surprise. The men seemed to react also to the fact that Telok looked Egyptian. This was much more than the men had expected, and the leader quickly started to backtrack. "Oh! Acts and Salmon… (Trying to laugh a little.) they are…"

Salmon looked into the man's eyes and said calmly, "You see, sir, we can't be last if we leave you behind. That would mean we are not doing our job for our captain. So, if you will please get moving, we would appreciate it."

The man shuffled his feet. "Certainly, we were through resting anyway." He turned, and the group of people began walking at a pace that neared a run.

Salmon watched them. "Why do they not see this as a miracle and a way of escape from the life of bondage?" he asked Joshua.

Joshua looked into Salmon's eyes and could see the sincerity of his heart. He was surprised that Salmon paid no attention to the fact they tried to talk down to him. He was more interested in their blindness. Telok began to teach, "Some people have no healthy concept of freedom, and they would rather live in what they know, instead of venturing out into something new and unknown. Their awareness of the Lord Most High has only begun to awaken, and we must be patient with them, just as the Lord is with us." He smiled at Salmon and put his hand on the younger boy's shoulder. "You handled that *very* well."

Salmon grinned at Telok and Acts. "Well, I had someone covering my back."

Joshua laughed. "Okay, let's get back to business."

Each one returned to his post, and as Joshua and Telok were walking together, Telok said, "They are quite the soldiers, aren't they?"

Joshua nodded, pleased. "That they are, my friend."

CHAPTER 12

Sin Stained Mud

As the tribe of Judah began the ascent up the east side of the Red Sea, the people could see where the opposite shoreline should be. Moses paused, his heart worried as he saw the tired faces of the people behind him, and he focused on the hill that led out of the sea. The Lord spoke to Moses' heart.

"It will not be far now. Keep the pace and keep moving. I will show you a rock on which you will stand with your arms outstretched so the children of Israel can look up at you and gain strength and courage. Do not be afraid, for I will bring glory to My Name and bless the children of Abraham, and they will know you are My servant."

Even Moses looked up the grade with pain in his own legs, and he spoke to the Lord confirming, "You are my strength and salvation."

Feeling a new strength wash over him, Moses kept the pace the Lord had set taking his first steps uphill with renewed determination.

~

The rear of the company neared the deepest part of the sea and would soon be moving uphill. Acts looked up and could see the wall of water was now taller than anything he had ever seen, even taller than the pyramids of Egypt. As Acts stopped to stare at the wall next to him, he began to fall. Salmon looked over in time to see Acts collapse and ran to his friend, signaling Joshua and shouting for Telok. By the time his three friends had reached him, Acts had fallen deeply into a dream.

~

Faces of Egyptians whirled past him. People that had held him in slavery all of his life were sinking into the ground. As Acts looked down, he noticed a stain on his hands. "Was it mud?" As Acts examined it more closely in the dream, he realized it was like blood, and it stank with the odor of death. Acts felt himself pulled to the ground. The stain changed from red to almost black, and the stench grew stronger, and he began to gag. Now crawling on his hands and knees, he saw small puddles of water that held scenes from his life, moments when he had made the decision to do the wrong thing on purpose: little lies told here and there, something he had taken without asking. He could see the attitude of his heart and it was black. Revelation dawned in his mind. Sin! It was sin in his life that stained his hands and stank so badly. He tried to stand, but something kept him weighed down. No matter how hard he struggled, he was forced to stay on his hands and knees in the dream. Was it the weight of slavery or the weight of his sin that held him down? Was there a difference? Water started rising all around him, and he knew if he did not get up, he would drown. As he crawled in an effort to stand up, he came to the scarred feet of the same warrior who had rescued him in his previous dream. As he looked up, he saw the warrior holding a lamb, and its blood was falling on Acts' hands. Acts saw that the lamb's blood was washing the stain from his hands. The warrior extended His right hand to Acts, and he saw again the scars in the hand of the warrior. Acts tried to glimpse the warrior's face, but it was like looking through water.

~

When Acts reached out to grasp the warrior's hand, the dream faded, and he realized it was the hands of Salmon and Joshua who reached for him. They sat him up slowly, and Joshua said, "Take in a deep breath, little brother. This sure is happening a lot lately. What does it all mean?"

Acts looked up into the face of his captain and things started to clear. "Did it last very long?" Acts asked.

Joshua nodded. "This was the longest. It lasted long enough for me and Telok to get to you from our positions after Salmon signaled for us. What did you see?"

"It was the warrior again," Acts replied.

"The same warrior with the scars?" asked Telok.

"Yes."

"Did you see his face this time?" asked Joshua.

"No. But it was the same man. He was holding a lamb, and the blood of the lamb was washing the stain from my hands."

"Stain?" interjected Salmon. "What stain?"

"I think it was the stain of my sin... but... maybe the stain of slavery... I'm not sure what it was, but the blood of the lamb was definitely washing my stain away."

Acts shook his head and rubbed his eyes. "I can't remember anymore right now."

Joshua patted Acts on the shoulder. "That's all right. Maybe you'll remember more later."

Some people near them had come over to offer assistance. Telok held up his hands and told them, "He's all right. He just looked up too long and fell over."

The people chuckled and turned around to continue their walk. Telok looked down at Acts with concern. "Do you feel like you can continue, or do you need some time to rest?"

Acts took in a deep, shaky breath and said, "I'm all right. I can go on now."

Salmon shook his head. "I don't think I'll ever get use to you doing this."

Acts smiled weakly at his friend. "How do you think I feel?"

Joshua and Telok pulled Acts to his feet, and the four turned to follow the company. Each one returned to their posts, but Acts felt troubled with the stain he had seen in his dream. *'Is this how I appear to You, Lord?'* he thought. *'I have never stopped to think of the cost of setting me free. The lamb I took care of for fourteen days; it was its innocence and its life the cost to set me free? Could the lamb in my dream be the lamb that saved me that night in Egypt when the Destroyer came and took all the firstborn? Is there a lamb also to take away my sin?'*

He scratched his head as he walked. *'I guess You, O Lord, will tell me what it all means someday.'*

The pillar of fire held the Egyptians at bay with the pillar of cloud stretched from Moses back over his men to the very back. The walk uphill had been grueling, and Moses wanted to stop and rest, but he knew in his heart he could not. He was not far from the rock the Lord had pointed out to him… if he stopped, others would want to stop, and that would be a costly mistake.

~

Joshua looked and could see the company beginning to reach the shoreline, where Moses stood on a rock. It seemed to be a very long way, especially with his head aching and legs burning. He studied the people as they walked. Most had their heads down and were simply trying to get through this ordeal. There were a few who walked with their heads up, marveling at the miracle around them. Joshua looked over at Salmon and could see him watching everything. Salmon was filled with wonder, just as Acts. Joshua turned to Telok and could see him looking at the miracle of the Lord as well, but he also noticed Telok glancing at Naoon. Joshua smiled in his heart. *'It would be nice to see Telok and Naoon becoming a couple.'* Then he shook his head and laughed out loud. "I'm no matchmaker."

Salmon turned his head toward Joshua. "What?"

Joshua looked at Salmon. "What?"

Salmon looked confused. "I thought you were talking to me."

"No… that was… I… never mind," Joshua said, with slight embarrassment.

Salmon looked at Joshua like the man was a bit crazy. "Okay…" and he turned away to study something, letting Joshua recover without scrutiny.

Telok walked up to the cart that carried Naoon and her baby girl. "Is everything okay?"

Telok followed her gaze. "Acts? He's fine. He just has these moments when he falls into a deep sleep. He doesn't know why. And in a few moments, he's up and going again."

Naoon nodded, looking thoughtful.

Telok decided to change the subject and shifted his weight. "How's your little girl?"

Naoon smiled at Telok. "She's full and sleeping now, thanks to you."

Telok turned a light shade of pink under his deeply tanned face, just visible in the dim light from the pillar of fire. "I haven't done anything, really."

"Of course, you have," Naoon insisted. "You found Guni and the cart to carry my daughter and me. You found rest for both of us and provided safety. I think you've done much, and I thank you… both of you." She looked at Guni, including him in her praise before turning back to Telok, "I think both of you are true gentlemen."

Telok noticed that Naoon made an effort to involve Guni in her commendations, and Telok was impressed she had done so. Telok smiled and drop back to walk behind the cart.

~

In an effort to take his mind off the distance remaining, Salmon walked over to Acts and began to talk with him.

"Have you remembered anything else from your dream?"

"No, not yet, but I will share with you when I do," came the reply of his friend.

Salmon smiled. "Good. Hey! Look at that big rock in the water!"

Acts turned to look at the large rock inside the wall of water. "I haven't seen a rock like that before."

Joshua joined them. "What are you doing?"

Acts pointed to the rock. "Look at that rock. It's a color and shape I've not seen." As he spoke, the rock suddenly moved. It began to unfold, and they realized what they had been looking at was only part of the body of a creature only talked about by sailors. Its neck stretched more than four horses long, and its tail extended even further. As it turned its head toward them, the mouth of this creature seemed large enough to swallow a full-grown cow. The three men started to back up, though it could not come out of the wall. Even so, it was still very frightening.

Salmon turned white. "What *is* that?"

The creature had two large flippers toward the front lower part of its body. The tail was long and heavy, and it narrowed with a flat end. The neck was large and thick, and the mouth was broad and filled with large teeth. The eyes were narrow and cat-like; their vertical pupils were black slits set in glowing yellow.

Telok glanced over and saw his three friends staring into the wall of water. Curious, he ran over to see what was so interesting. As he moved to run, Naoon and Guni followed him with their eyes to see where Telok was headed. Naoon spotted the creature and gasped quietly. Guni stared in surprise as he saw it, too.

"Do you see that?" Naoon asked Guni quietly.

Guni nodded. "I see it, but I don't know what it is."

Naoon's brow knitted in worry, and she spoke in a low voice, more to herself than anyone else, "Don't get too close, Telok."

The creature turned to face the people in their trek across the sea floor and swam lazily in front of them, showing off his impressive physique.

Salmon gazed in amazement. "It has to be at least sixty feet long, and the belly looks like it could hold a couple of cows at one time."

The four had not noticed several people who had slowed to watch the creature with them. As the creature passed by, they backed up from the wall as well. No one said a word as they stood in astonishment. It made one pass by the last tribe before swimming north into the sea.

Telok shook his head. "I have heard some of the sailors tell of a creature they called 'Leviathan' or 'the gliding serpent' that destroyed ships at sea. I always doubted the story until now, but I would believe something that big could indeed take a ship down."

Acts looked at Joshua and grinned. "I've never seen one of those in my dreams before, but I guess I will now."

That brought a chuckle from everyone who stopped to see the creature. Joshua turned to look up the path and could see the first tribes were almost to the top of the hill on the way out of the sea. The climb was steep, and the animals had to work at pulling the carts up the grade. He turned to his companions. "We don't have far to go. Keep everyone moving; don't slow the pace. We have to reach the other side as soon as we can."

His companions nodded and ran off to hurry things along. Telok returned to his position by Naoon and she asked, "What was that, Telok?"

"I've only heard of the story from sailors. They called it 'Leviathan' when it was told. It was always said to be the most feared creature of the sea, and now I can see why."

"I'm glad you did not go very close."

"Oh? And why is that?"

She smiled shyly. "I wouldn't want anything to happen to my guardian."

Telok returned her smile. "I thank you for your concern."

"I'm glad you didn't get too close, either" Guni added.

"And I thank you, as well," Telok replied.

~

Everyone walked for a long while without saying a word. Moses had reached a large rock on which he would stand, where he would be able to see the entire company, and they could see him. Joshua sighed and considered the distance traveled thus far. He estimated 11 or 12 miles, at the very least, with probably seven or eight still to go. It had been the most difficult task he had ever experienced. Never had he walked so far in one day at such a speed. Several days had passed since he had been able to rest for even one full night. His stomach rumbled and his throat was dry. He spotted a water cart and directed his steps for it. A young girl walked next to it, and seeing Joshua, she asked, "May I draw some water for you, Joshua?"

He smiled at her and said, "That would be very kind of you. Do I look as thirsty as I feel?"

She laughed. "You look very thirsty."

Joshua laughed with her, taking the cup from her hands.

A moment of silence passed as Joshua drained the container. "Will it be much longer?" she finally asked.

Joshua returned the cup to her. "Not too much longer: Maybe six miles or so. That's not long when you consider how far we have come."

She nodded. "The water is getting very low."

Joshua immediately felt a slight anxiety. "How low?" he asked.

"Less than a few large pitchers," she replied.

Joshua had not thought about the water supply since Telok had mentioned it quite a while before. It would be the next concern after crossing the sea. He thanked the young girl, saying, "Take courage, little sister. The Lord has set us free, and you will grow up in a whole new life."

Joshua considered his last statement to the young girl: *'You will grow up in a whole new life.'* What an awesome thought.

~

Acts and Salmon continued to walk together. "It's kind of funny," Acts remarked. "Even though we are where the Lord has led us and we are doing what He has commanded, I feel out of place, almost to the point of being lost."

Salmon looked at his friend. "I have been feeling the same way, but I didn't want to say anything. I thought I was the only one."

Acts nodded. "We are walking into a life that totally depends on the God of Abraham. He is leading us, just as He led our forefather. I feel uneasy, but at peace also. It's really strange."

"Well, I certainly don't know how to explain it," stated Salmon. The boys walked and laughed, sharing the thoughts and feelings they had. But when they really started to think about what they had said, they found themselves realizing Abraham might have felt the same way.

~

The first six tribes had now reached the rock where Moses stood and were beginning to form a half-moon on the shoreline behind him.

It had been a very difficult walk, and Acts turned to gaze upon the fiery miracle of the Lord, which held the Egyptians at bay. He suddenly realized that the pillar of fire was not only, holding the Egyptians back, but it was the light by which they walked. As he looked at the pillar his focus changed, he noticed a cloud of dust in the distance and a sound like thunder coming from behind them. He squinted his eyes to try and see the source. "What do you suppose is causing all that? I have never heard that sound from either of the pillars."

The Egyptians looked at the pillar of fire a different way; they saw the pillar of fire as something, their god, Ra, would do, so that they would be able to see and capture and kill the Hebrews.

Salmon turned to look, and as he did, he caught the attention of Joshua and Telok. All four stood looking back. Joshua suddenly realized the cause of the sound. The pillar of fire was advancing, and the Egyptians were now charging full force toward the Hebrews.

Telok turned quickly to Joshua. "What do we do now, my captain?"

Joshua turned to look at the rock where Moses stood, then at the distance between them, he estimated the time needed to reach him. It was not enough. The last part of the climb was steep, and everyone teetered on the brink of exhaustion. With the Egyptian chariots closing in, he thought, '*Now, the fight begins.*'

Act examined their situation and remembered one of his dreams where he could see the Lord God coming to their aid. He prayed in his heart, '*Lord, You, have brought us so far. I know You will protect us from the enemy who wants to destroy us.*'

Satan had witnessed the power of the Lord in Egypt, but he now had given the Egyptians a strong desire to take revenge and re-capture the slaves. He moved around the Pharaoh, giving him the idea: "The slaves are gone! Who will do the work now? You need the slaves, but not all of them. You can kill as many as you like. Take them!"

Pharaoh pondered on the thoughts and as he led his army to Migdol, the thirst for blood only built in his heart. He had his army in chase, and he would teach the Hebrews a lesson and put them back under his thumb.

Other people started to notice the sound, and they turned around to investigate. When they saw the pillar of fire advancing rapidly toward them and the cloud of dust from the chariots behind it, mass panic broke out. People screamed and tried to run up the hill to Moses. As hard as the people worked, they were still losing ground, and the Egyptians were quickly closing the space between them. Acts cried out loud, "Lord! You are our protection! Save us!"

CHAPTER 13

TURN TO FIGHT

THE EGYPTIAN GENERAL LEADING THE attack pressed his driver hard to close the distance to the Hebrews. His hate and desire to punish totally consumed his heart. There were more than 600 chariots, each carrying two or three soldiers. Countless foot soldiers ran behind the horses. The thirst for battle and blood in every heart fueled their energy for the long dash. The Egyptians detested this God of Israel who had brought such misery to Egypt, and they wanted revenge. Now, it looked as if they would have it.

The last of the tribes were now running the final mile to the rock where Moses stood. The tribes on the beach behind Moses saw their brothers and sisters rushing toward them, but they did not know why until one young man ran up to Moses, crying, "The Egyptians are coming!"

During the walk, down the path through the sea, time had felt so distant. It seemed a lifetime ago they had felt the whip from the slave master's hand, smelled the stink of mud mixed with hay, or the weight of bricks on their backs, carrying the stones to build houses for an ungrateful and unforgiving nation.

As the last two tribes sprinted with all the strength they had left, the soldiers under Joshua's command worked hard picking up those being left behind. No sooner had Acts picked one person up and got them running again, another would fall, and it was the same for Salmon, Joshua, and Telok. Each breath burned in their lungs, and they felt as if the next breath would not come. Telok ran up to Guni and took him by the shoulders and said, "Take Naoon and the baby as fast as you can. Keep the cart close to the wall on the right. There you will find the clearest path to the rock where Moses stands. Place the cart behind Moses. Stay as close to him as you can. You will have to help her climb with the baby. There is where I hope to meet you."

Guni looked at Naoon, and in the direction of the Egyptians, and back to Telok. He brought himself up to his full height. "We will be there waiting for you."

"Good! Now, go!"

As Guni prepared to move the oxen to the wall, Naoon held out her hand. Telok took it, and she said, "Remember, I need my guardian."

Telok smiled and slowed his run, releasing her hand, and time seemed to slow as he watched her being taken away, in his heart knowing that if it came to battle, he would not see her again. He now ran to Joshua. There needed to be a plan, and there was very little time to prepare. He turned one more time to look at Naoon, his heart mounting with passion to fight to the death while protecting her and her baby.

He heard Joshua's voice. "Telok! We've got to get these people to the beach!" Joshua shouted over the roar of the people and the Egyptians. "The Egyptians will certainly be hurting by the time they reach the edge of the beach, and most of the company will have had time to recover from the climb."

Acts and Salmon ran up to meet them.

"We will run with these last members of the tribe past the edge of the beach."

Joshua commanded. "We will stop and turn to lead in the fight. We do not have time to do anything else." He looked into the eyes of each man. Acts and Salmon were so young and yet so full of courage, exactly what was needed to face such an ominous opponent.

He looked at Telok and knew they would stand together in battling to the death.

Joshua looked back at Acts and Salmon and said grimly, "They will seek Telok and me to kill first. We will stand as one unit, our backs together. We will take their weapons from them and use them against them. I don't know why the Lord has chosen this place for the battle, but it looks like we will be at the hottest point. We must trust Him."

He did not really know what else to say. A brief silence fell over the unit before Telok put his hand on Joshua's arm. "It will be done as you have said, my captain."

Acts and Salmon nodded to Joshua. "We stand with you."

Joshua breathed deeply. "Good. Let's get these people to the rock where Moses stands."

The formation of people running had formed a tear drop shape. The body of the tear drop was in the center of the path, with the tip of the tear drop reaching the beach. Joshua's warriors were pushing the children of Israel to keep running. Each man turned and started picking people up, pushing them to reach the mark. Telok glanced up the hill and could see Guni with the cart. They were not far now, and Telok felt confident they would make it.

Pharaoh stood in the tower of Migdol watching his army. Not yet realized by him, but the Lord was giving him the vision and capability, to see and hear all that was going on across the sea.

The tribes standing on the beach ran out to help gather the people, and the fighting line formed along the front of the shoreline. A slaughter awaited them, but the children of Israel stood ready to fight, in order to protect their families.

Moses stood with his arms outstretched, his staff in his right hand. He said nothing as Joshua and his three worked with all their strength.

The Egyptians were now within sight. The front line was made up of the very best warriors and chariots. It was a sea of spears, bows, and swords in the hands of war-crazed men seeking blood to avenge the death of their firstborns in Egypt.

Joshua turned to estimate how much time they had to get the people to the mark. The distance of the run was too far. They wouldn't make it. He estimated about 20,000 people still remaining on the path. The fight would begin here. He slowed his run to get ready for the battle. As he turned to face the enemy, he saw one of the chariot's wheels spin off and jam the chariot next to it. Another wheel popped off, and then another. Joshua turned an incredulous look toward Moses. "Keep going!" he yelled to his companions. "The Lord is giving us time!"

The Egyptians had slowed so much they stood almost completely still, stumbling over the broken chariots and dodging the fleeing horses.

The pillar of fire now moved over the Hebrews, and it made its transformation to the pillar of cloud. The sun began to peak over the horizon Moses watched his men intently. They still did not understand, the Egyptians they see today, they will never see again.

The last of the people were reaching the beach, Joshua put Telok to his right and Acts and Salmon on his left.

"Joshua!" Moses shouted. "Get the men back! Push them behind me! No one is to be left in front of me!"

Joshua did not understand the orders, but he did as he was commanded. He turned to his men and gave the order to push everyone back behind Moses. People were confused and upset; the threat of mass hysteria so close that Joshua almost succumbed to it himself.

The chariots had created such a line of confusion the foot soldiers were having a hard time getting past them, and the entire Egyptian army now stretched from the middle of the sea to within a few hundred yards of the Hebrews. They were close enough that the people could see their faces.

"Joshua," Moses said calmly. The Lord carried Moses' voice to his servant. "Joshua, bring your men up to the rock and stand beside me."

Joshua gave the orders, and Acts, Salmon, and Telok followed him to stand with Moses and Aaron. Telok was climbing up around the edge of the rock when he spotted Naoon and the baby with Guni holding the oxen at the cart. Telok asked Joshua if he could stand with them.

Joshua nodded. "Stand with them. They will need you close, only be sure you can see what Moses wants you to see."

Moses had no fear in his eyes, no panic. Joshua, Acts, and Salmon marveled at their leader's serenity. Aaron walked over to Joshua and handed him the two ram's horns that had been used to signal the company before, and Moses said, "Take the horns, and give the signal for silence."

Pharaoh could see the trouble his army was having. He shouted to Ra, his god, to give his army victory. He would not bow his knee to this Hebrew god. He would see his god, come to their aid.

Joshua handed the horns to Acts and Salmon. The boys took the horns with a mixture of pride, fear, and trust. Drawing in a nervous breath, they sounded the signal, and the entire company of Israel became silent.

Moses faced the people, his back to the enemy. His arms outstretched.

By this point, such fear and confusion had woven its way through the Egyptians their advancement had come to a halt. The infantry broke formation and began running back toward the west shore, some crying out "Run away from the Israelites! Their Lord is fighting for them!"

Moses spoke to the children of Israel in the same, calm manner. "Do not be afraid. Stand firm, and you will see the deliverance of the Lord today. The Egyptians you see today you will never see again."

The Lord said to Moses, **"Stretch out your hands over the sea."**

Moses faced the path and the walls of water. The miracle of the Lord brought a fear to the children of Israel, such they had never known before.

CHAPTER 14

ENEMIES CRUSHED

FEAR PARALYZED THE EGYPTIANS. THE General was shouting orders, the soldiers were trying to get the wheels back on the chariots, and the foot soldiers were running as fast as they could back to the west side of the sea.

The Hebrews stood silent, watching in fear as the most revered army on the Earth fled before them. Their ranks were disordered, and the command chain had collapsed. Moses raised his hands, each reaching toward a wall of water.

Acts looked out over the path, and above the Egyptians, he could see the snake of mist circling over the army of Egypt. It paused and seemed to look right at Acts. He saw the Destroyer smile in the moment of its harvest.

Acts was the only one seeing the creature. He had seen it once more, face to face and he remembered how terrified he was. Now, he wasn't afraid. He knew the Lord would protect him.

Moses now closed his arms together over the water as the Lord had commanded him and, as he did, Acts watched the walls of water start to fall in from the top. The sound was deafening, and the ground shook violently. The Hebrews watched in fear and amazement as the walls of water fell on the Egyptians, crushing them and smashing their chariots and horses. Everything was destroyed. With no survivors, the snake mist was gone, carrying with it the souls of every man covered by the sea. The Hebrews watched and, after a moment, they could see the bodies of the Egyptians being pushed around by the water.

Salmon stared at the bodies floating in the water, and then suddenly grabbed Acts' arm. "Look! It is the Egyptian who caused the death of my brother!" he exclaimed.

Acts looked to where Salmon pointed and watched the body rise and fall with the waves. Acts remained silent but stood with his friend in a moment of uncertain feelings.

~

Pharaoh collapsed to his knees on the west bank of the Red Sea in total despair and unbelief. He watched his entire army be destroyed before his eyes. The waters gracefully and powerfully fell back into place, claiming everything remaining in its path as its own. Pharaoh saw the serpentine cloud that had visited his house and taken the life of his first-born sons. It coiled out of the water, and Pharaoh's blood ran cold with fear as it hovered in front of him. It emanated death, especially as it carried with it the souls of his army. With a loud hiss, it pushed hard into the earth and vanished. Pharaoh finally realized the price of his stubbornness: his son, his army, his kingdom. The Lord God had finally crushed the stone-cold heart of the king of Egypt.

Acts looked across the sea with a vision he did not realize; he was seeing the face of the Pharaoh. The Egyptian king looked in disbelief at the destruction of his entire army. No battle had ever taken so many live at one time, within only a few minutes. Act watched his lips, and the Lord allowed him to hear the Pharaoh: "Oh! That I would have listened." It was the saddest thing Acts ever heard in his life.

On the east side of the Red Sea, the children of Israel stood utterly silent in awe. After 430 years to the day prophesied by Joseph, the Lord God of Abraham had finally freed the Israelites from their slavery. No one now doubted the great power of the Lord. The people now feared and trusted Him and his servant, Moses.

For a long time, the people just stared at the water. After a few minutes, Miriam, Moses' sister, picked up a tambourine and began to dance and sing praises to the Lord. Her voice sounded pure and clear. Moses joined her, and the people took their cue. Moses and Miriam alternated singing a verse and the people sang the refrain back to them. Their voices could be heard throughout the whole camp. Music and praise filled the camp with joy, and it was very pleasing to the Lord.

Salmon looked around at the men he served with in the light of the morning, realizing the position he now held in the company was in service to Joshua and Moses. Great peace settled in his heart with this knowledge. The friendship that had been built with Acts, Telok, and Joshua would last the rest of his life.

Telok had eyes only for Naoon and her baby girl. His heart saw the new life before him and the endless possibilities in it. He could not explain what he was feeling for the young woman, but he knew, they had been brought into his life for a reason and he thanked the Lord.

Joshua searched the sea one more time before turning back to the company. Klee was making her way to him. Joshua thanked the Lord God for the privilege of his wedding and the future he would have with Klee.

Acts had seen his visions come to pass and felt peace in his heart. He now had a new family and a place of service with Joshua and Moses.

Hearing his name called, Salmon turned back to Acts, and they looked at the sea again. Neither of them said anything, just took in the sight of the water and the people.

~

The Lord spoke to Moses, **"Lead the people from the Red Sea and travel into the Desert of Shur for three days. I will show you the way."**

Moses replied to the Lord, "Lord God of Abraham, we are out of water."

"I know My friend, My servant, Moses; I AM will provide."

Moses smiled as a great peace blanketed his whole being, and his worry immediately vanished. "Yes, Lord," he agreed quietly. "You provide everything."

Salmon turned to Acts and asked, "So, where do you think we go from here?" As he looked into the eyes of his friend, he could see Acts' eyes were wide open as he raised his hand to his ear. Salmon immediately reached out to grab him. Acts closed his eyes and Salmon lowered him to the ground.

In the mind of Acts, he could see people staggering in a land. Wind blowing dust all around. Children looked like they were crying, but they made no sound. Acts could see several wells where water should have been. He realized the people were dying of thirst…